INVASION OF THE
DOGNAPPERS

Patrick Jennings

SCHOLASTIC INC.
New York Toronto London Auckland
Sydney Mexico City New Delhi Hong Kong

ISBN 978-0-545-49251-5

Copyright © 2012 by Patrick Jennings.
All rights reserved. Published by Scholastic Inc., 557 Broadway, New York, NY 10012,
by arrangement with Egmont USA. SCHOLASTIC and associated logos
are trademarks and/or registered trademarks of Scholastic Inc.

12 11 10 9 8 7 6 5 4 3 2 1   12 13 14 15 16 17/0

Printed in the U.S.A.   40

First Scholastic printing, September 2012

For Logan and Blake,
who heard it first

Thanks to Heather Flanagan;
Cassie, River, Rowan, and Shae;
and Lily Richey, for the title.

Contents

1. The First Dog

"Stop the bus! Stop the bus! A dog just vanished into thin air!"

The bus driver, who wore a black sea captain's cap down low over her eyes, looked up at the huge, rectangular mirror over her head and said, "Sit down, Logan."

Logan was bouncing on his seat.

"Roberta! I think it was abducted by aliens!" he yelled louder. "You must stop the bus!"

"You will be very sorry if I stop this bus, Logan," the driver said. "Now sit down."

Logan groaned his disapproval, then plopped onto his seat. He pressed his face to the window, hoping to catch a glimpse of the thief.

2. Poof!

"I saw a dog vanish this morning," Logan said.

"What do you mean 'vanish'?" Thatcher asked, flipping his shoulder-length hair out of his face. "Did it run away? Did someone take it?"

"It was tied up outside Sandwiches," Logan said. "Then it vanished."

"A dog vanished," Kian said flatly. The only sign that he found this remark absurd was the slight cocking of his left eyebrow. Unfortunately, his bangs hid his eyebrows.

"Right," Logan said. "Poof."

"Can a dog vanish?" Thatcher asked. "I mean, into thin air? They can't, right? Can they?"

"What about when they get picked up by the dogcatcher?" Aggy asked, looking up from her book, the third in a series about a girl who discovers Earth is actually the blue eye of a giant being.

"That's not vanishing," Kian said. "That's getting arrested."

"Captured, more like," Aggy said, and looked back at her book. Aggy couldn't abide inaccuracy.

"This dog vanished," Logan said. "Poof."

"How do you know its owner didn't just leave with it?" Thatcher asked, shaking his head. This caused his long, sandy-colored hair to fall back into his face. He tossed it away. "How do you know it didn't just get loose and run away?"

"Oh, maybe because the collar and leash were still there," Logan answered.

"They were?" Thatcher asked, with a little gasp.

"The collar was lying on the sidewalk, still buckled, and still connected to the leash, and the leash was still tied to the STOP sign," Logan said.

Thatcher stared off into space, his eyelids sliding down to half mast, contemplating this.

"I was standing there, waiting for the bus," Logan said, "and this dog was sitting there, whining for his owner. *Unnnh, unnnh, unnnh . . .*"

"Whose dog was it?" Thatcher asked. "Wasn't he there? Did anyone else see what happened?"

"I don't know, but let me finish, will you? So the dog's whining outside Sandwiches—*unnnh, unnnh, unnnh*—and this guy walks up, pets it for a minute, gives it a dog treat, then goes into the store. The dog stopped whining when the guy was petting him, but started whining again when the guy left. *Unnnh, unnnh—*"

"Enough with the whining, Logan," Aggy said.

"Who was the guy?" Thatcher asked. "Did you know him? What did he look like?"

Thatcher often asked questions in clusters.

"Let me finish, will you?" Logan said, glaring.

"Sorry," Thatcher said. Hair flip. "Go on. Sorry."

"So the bus pulls up, right? I get on and find a seat, then look out the window, and poof!—the dog's gone. All that's left is the collar and the leash. Okay?" He shook his head impatiently.

"You think the guy came out and took it?" asked Thatcher.

"I doubt he came out of the store, undid the dog's collar, rebuckled the collar, and then ran off with the dog that fast," Logan said.

"What about someone else then?" Thatcher asked.

"I didn't see anyone else."

"Of course you didn't," Kian said. "You were at Sandwiches, and there's never anyone going in and out of Sandwiches."

This was more sarcasm. Sandwiches was a busy neighborhood grocery and deli. Kian delighted in saying the opposite of what he meant.

"Even if it wasn't that guy," Thatcher said, "*some*body took the dog. The owner wouldn't leave his dog's collar and leash behind."

"Maybe she couldn't untie her own knot," Aggy said, her eyes still trained on the pages of her book. Aggy had fine, cornsilk hair she usually wore braided and bound at the back of her head. Wispy bangs reached down to her dark eyebrows, which often telegraphed her emotions. In this case, her brows twisted in bored exasperation.

"Listen," Logan said, growing more frustrated by the moment. "The owner couldn't have come out and tried to untie the leash from the bike rack, then unbuckled the collar and rebuckled it and taken the dog away, all in the time it took me to get on the bus and sit down and look out the window. No way. It happened too fast. I saw the dog tied to the rack when I got on the bus, and then when I sat down, it was gone. Poof. Vanished."

"Can you stop saying 'poof'?" Aggy asked. "It's kind of driving me nuts."

"I say somebody kidnapped the dog," Thatcher said. "Right?"

"You mean 'dognapped,'" Aggy said.

"Dognapped all right," Logan said. "But not by a person."

"Huh?" Thatcher asked. "Not by a person? What does that mean? You don't think it was a human being that napped the dog?"

"Nope."

Aggy looked up. "You think it was an alien, don't you?"

"Yes, I do."

Everyone groaned.

"It must have been," Logan said. "What else could make a dog vanish? There's no other explanation."

"No other explanation," Kian said.

"Aliens are always your explanation," Thatcher said.

"I'm telling you, an alien beamed that dog right out of his collar," Logan said.

"Why would an alien steal a dog?" Aggy asked.

"Maybe he loves dogs," Thatcher said. "I do."

"I bet he loves them all right," Logan said. "I bet he loves them for breakfast."

"That's just gross," Aggy said.

"You guys are discussing your group project, right?" asked Nathan, their teacher, coming over.

Aggy closed her book.

"Group project?" Thatcher asked, tossing his hair. "Do we have to do a group project? I don't remember you telling us about a group project."

Kian elbowed him. "Sure, Nathan. That's exactly what we're discussing. We're discussing our group project."

"So what's it going to be?" Nathan asked, scratching his untrimmed black beard. "A skit? A model? A game?"

Simultaneously, Kian said, "Skit," Thatcher said, "Game," and Aggy said, "Model."

Nathan smiled. "Sounds like you have more discussing to do. That's fine, but don't waste time. It's time to produce." He raised his arm, pointed at the ceiling, and repeated in a deep, theatrical voice, "Produce!"

"Nathan," Logan said, "you believe in alien abduction, don't you?"

"I don't know, Logan," Nathan said, bringing his hand down and resting it on the back of Logan's chair. "I suppose none of us know."

"I do," Logan said. "I saw one today."

"All right, Logan," Nathan said. "But for now let's focus on your astronomy project, okay?"

"That's kind of hard, Nathan," Logan said, "considering what I saw today."

"Well, please try," Nathan said, and walked away.

3. A Serious Alien Presence

"An alien abducted a dog today outside Sandwiches," Logan told his mom after he got in the car.

"Uh-huh," his mom said, putting the car into reverse.

"Or probably aliens, plural. I doubt one would travel across the universe by itself. What if it got sick or something, or had to go to the bathroom during a meteor shower? Who would steer? Autopilot probably wouldn't work in a meteor shower...."

"Logan, I have a lot on my mind right now," his mom said. "Patrice can't babysit this week. She had to leave town unexpectedly."

"But, Mom. I saw a dog abducted by—"

"Aliens. I heard you, Logan. I'm listening to you. I'm just asking if it can wait till we get home."

"I've waited to talk to you about it all day. If you would get me a cell phone, I could have called you. Or texted you. But you won't."

"You're ten, Logan."

"Ten and a sixth. And I don't see what difference that makes. You know I'm very mature for my age."

"Yes, sweetheart, you are very mature," his mom said, then smiled at him over her shoulder. Logan sat in the backseat beside his little brother, Sloane, who was strapped into his car seat.

"I agree it wouldn't make good sense to get Sloane a cell," Logan said. "He doesn't even talk good."

Sloane looked at him. "Goga," he said.

"See?" Logan said. "He still calls me Goga. Even after all the years he's known me."

"Less than two years, Logan," his mom said with a smile.

"A year and seven-twelfths. I wouldn't support getting Sloane a cell phone. But I'm mature enough to have one. I sure could have used one today. When I informed Roberta that a dog had been abducted, she wouldn't even stop the bus. If I had a cell, I could have called nine-one-one. Or the FBI."

"Roberta has a lot of responsibility, Logan. Maybe an abducted dog isn't as important as getting a busload of kids to school on time. I bet she reported the incident when she got back to the bus barn."

"Doubtful," Logan said. "She's never reported any of the abductions and sightings I've witnessed. In my opinion, she doesn't take alien presence on Earth seriously enough. Don't they ask her about such things during the bus-driver interview process?"

"I'm not sure, Logan."

"You need to go over her head, Mom. Contact the president, maybe, or the head of the FBI. Though I bet they already know about it. I've heard the FBI knows there are aliens on Earth, but they don't tell us because they think we'll panic. I wouldn't panic."

"I'm sure you wouldn't."

"I didn't panic today. If the FBI knows there

are aliens and they're monitoring them, fine. But I don't think they should allow aliens to steal people's dogs. I sure don't want one to steal Bubba."

The family's aged pet bloodhound was resting behind the backseat in the cargo area.

"*Unnnh, unnnh, unnnh,*" whined Sloane.

"That's right, Sloanie," Logan's mom said. "That's what Bubba says."

"Bubba fart!" Sloane said, slapping his chubby palms on the plastic tray in from of him.

"Yup," his mom said. "Bubba farts all right."

"It's not her fault, Sloane," Logan said. "She's old. You'll probably fart, too, when you're as old as Bubba."

"Sloanie farts now," his mom said, peering at Sloane in her rearview mirror.

"Sloanie fart!" Sloane said, and, again, pounded his tray.

"Yeah, you fart, Sloane," Logan said, "but not as much as Bubba."

"Which is why we never have to worry about aliens taking her."

"I hope you're right, Mom." Logan turned and stared vaguely out the window. "I hope you're right."

4. Confidential

Logan woke up an hour earlier than usual the next morning.

"Aliens," he reminded himself.

He flung back the covers and leaped into his slippers.

"Must thwart the aliens."

He tugged off his pajamas and pulled on the T-shirt, jeans, and socks he had taken off the night before.

Bubba climbed down slowly from Logan's bed, stretched, yawned, then farted.

"Oh, man, Bubba," Logan said, waving the air away from his nose with his hand. "That's brutal."

His mom was in the kitchen, in her robe and slippers, holding a steaming mug up under her nose.

"What are you doing up so early?" she asked.

"What do you think?" he said. "I'm going on alien patrol."

"At six thirty in the morning?"

"I'm going to stake out Sandwiches. I have a hunch the alien will come back for more dogs."

His mom nodded her sleepy head. "Okay. But don't go anywhere but Sandwiches. And don't talk to anyone you don't know."

"Yeah, I know, Mom," Logan said as he stuffed binoculars, his digital camera, and a clipboard into his backpack.

"You must eat breakfast first, Logan. And I haven't packed your lunch yet. I haven't even gotten a *hug* yet."

Logan walked over and gave her one. He didn't put his all into it.

"That was sad," his mom said.

"Sorry, Mom. Real hugs will have to wait till the extraterrestrials are apprehended."

"Sit, son," his mom said, standing. "I'm making you some eggs and toast."

Logan dropped into the chair. "You don't get how important this is, obviously."

"Eating is important. You're growing. And you can't fight aliens on an empty stomach."

"You always say that."

"Because it's true. I happen to know that all FBI agents eat a substantial, nutritious breakfast every morning before going out to hunt down extraterrestrials."

Logan glared at her, his pale brown eyes narrowing, his freckles gathering around his nose.

His mom glared back with the same pale brown eyes. She had the freckles, too, though hers were fainter. She didn't get outside as often as her son.

"Do any of your clients work for the FBI?" Logan asked.

"You know I can't breach client confidentiality," his mom answered as she flicked on a burner. "But yes."

"FBI agents need life coaches?"

"More than anybody," his mom said, opening the fridge and removing a gray carton of eggs. "And don't forget about the guy I dated in college who worked for the FBI's special ET task force. The ETTF."

"How did you know he worked for the ETTF? Don't FBI agents take vows of confidentiality, too?"

"I have ways of finding things out," his mom said with a grin. "Over easy?"

"Over fast. I'm in a hurry."

"Okay, but the yolk might break, and you don't like it when the yolk runs."

"I'll risk it," Logan said.

"If you want speedy, why don't you help by getting out the bread and start making your sandwich?"

"Yes, Coach."

"That does it. Hit the floor! Fifty push-ups!"

Logan knew she was joking, but he fell onto his palms on the floor anyway.

"Get up, nut job, and make your sandwich," his mom said.

5. The Second Dog

Logan walked the few blocks to Sandwiches Market, which had been in the neighborhood for more than a hundred years. He stopped across the street, hid behind the dogwood on the library's lawn, and prepared for his surveillance. This meant removing from his backpack his binoculars and camera and hanging them around his neck, taking out a pair of black sunglasses with black lenses and putting them on, and unpacking a mechanical pencil and a clipboard. He glanced at his watch and, as he couldn't read the LED display, lifted the dark glasses to his forehead.

"Seven thirty-four," he said softly, then pulled the glasses back down over his eyes and recorded the time on the clipboard. Beside it he wrote "Sandwiches" and the weather conditions: "Gray.

Breezy." He did some quick figuring in his head, then muttered, "Fifty-one minutes before the bus comes."

He raised the binoculars to his eyes. They clinked on his sunglasses.

"Dumb glasses," he muttered, taking them off, folding them, and balancing them on a low branch of the tree. He then peered through the binoculars at the scene in front of Sandwiches.

People came and went on foot, by bicycle, in cars and trucks. The customers entered the store empty-handed and emerged with groceries, newspapers, and, especially, white paper coffee cups with black plastic tops that had a small sipping hole through which steam escaped. Some of the customers also held muffins, croissants, or bagels with cream cheese and alternated between biting and sipping.

People left their dogs outside on the sidewalk, tied to a pole or a sign or the bike rack; some trusted their dogs and left them untied. Some of the dogs sat on the sidewalk and calmly waited. Some squirmed and whined. Some wagged their tails when people stopped to say hello.

(These people usually spoke to the dogs in high-pitched baby talk.) Some of the dogs licked hands with their long, wet tongues. Some licked themselves, right there on one of Nelsonport's busiest corners.

Logan recorded it all. Every person, every dog, every bagel, every detail. He put the time beside each observation.

He was hoping to observe the man he'd seen the day before, the man who had petted the dog just before it vanished. Logan had noticed some distinctive traits in the man: he had spoken to the dog with an unfamiliar accent; he carried dog treats; and he was hairy. Very hairy. Hairy face. Hairy neck. Hairy hands.

To his disappointment, Logan did not see a hairy, accented man carrying dog treats in the fifty-one minutes he cased Sandwiches.

When his bus eventually pulled to the curb, it took Logan a few seconds before he realized he was not standing where he should be.

"Wait! Roberta, wait!" he yelled, and bolted for the bus without bothering to stow his gear. His camera and binoculars bounced on his belly;

his unzipped backpack banged against his back. He clutched his clipboard and mechanical pencil in his hands.

It wasn't until he was on the bus and blocks away from Sandwiches that he realized what he'd left behind.

"Stop the bus!" he yelled. "Stop the bus! I left my sunglasses on the branch!"

"Sit down, Logan," Roberta said, eyeing him in her big mirror.

🐾 🐾 🐾

Logan's friends were clustered together outside their classroom, excitedly talking.

"What's going on?" Logan asked, penetrating the group. "What happened?"

Everyone immediately stopped talking and stared at him.

"You guys talking about me or something?" Logan asked.

They continued to stare, which caused Logan to lose his patience.

"Tell me what's going on right now," he demanded. "Right now. Tell me."

"Kian's mom's dog's disappeared." Thatcher said, and patted Kian on the back sympathetically.

"It's just Chloe," Kian said.

They all knew Chloe, the pint-size, yapping Yorkie Kian's mom toted around like a teddy bear. She was not the group's favorite pooch.

Logan pulled his clipboard out of his bag, and asked Kian, "When was she last seen?"

"I don't know," Kian said. "Last night? I was at my dad's house. My mom called my dad about it and he told me."

"Any suspicious characters seen lingering about?" Logan asked after writing "Chloe" and the previous day's date on his chart.

"You mean aliens?" Kian asked. "Were there any aliens about?"

"Precisely," Logan said, not catching Kian's mocking tone.

"I forgot to ask my mom about it," Kian said, continuing to pretend he was taking Logan seriously.

Thatcher wasn't fooled. He and Kian had been best friends a long time.

"Come on, Kian, you got to admit that it's weird your mom's dog disappeared."

"There's no proof the dog at Sandwiches was stolen," Aggy interrupted. "Or even missing. And we don't know whose dog it was, so we can't find out."

"I didn't see the owner," Logan grumbled. "But I did see the dog disappear, Aggy."

"Just because it wasn't there anymore when you looked out the bus window doesn't mean it disappeared."

"What about the collar and leash?" Logan asked.

"Yeah!" Thatcher said.

"How do we know they belonged to that dog?" Aggy asked. "Maybe they'd been lying there all along."

"Yeah," Kian said. "Probably from some other dog that got beamed up."

"Dude, you are wicked!" Thatcher laughed, and lunged at Kian.

Because Kian was shorter, he ducked Thatcher easily. He then tried to scoot away, but Thatcher twisted and caught Kian in a headlock. Kian bent at the waist, catching Thatcher off balance and lifting him off his feet. He wasn't strong enough to hold the much bigger boy, however, and they both crashed to the ground.

"It was the same collar and leash," Logan said, oblivious to them. "The dog was dognapped, and so was Chloe."

"How do you know that?" Aggy asked.

"I know aliens," Logan said.

Everybody groaned, even Kian and Thatcher, who were wrestling in the grass.

"I'm going to investigate Chloe's abduction," Logan said, slipping his clipboard back into his bag. "If anyone wants to assist me, let me know before the end of class." Then he walked away.

6. The Intergalactic Canine Rescue Unit

"Did you see anyone peculiar hanging around your house?" Logan asked Kian's mom.

She looked at her son, who, with Thatcher and Aggy, had come along on Logan's investigation.

"Peculiar?" she asked Logan. She glanced at the binoculars and camera that hung around his neck, his clipboard and pen, and, perched atop his head, his dark glasses, which he had retrieved from the dogwood tree. "No," she said. "I didn't see anyone peculiar."

"No one new to the neighborhood?" Logan went on. "No strange men? No hairy ones?"

"Hairy?" Aggy asked, looking up from her book.

"No, Logan," Kian's mom said, eyeing Logan skeptically. "I didn't see any hairy men."

Logan scribbled a note. "When was the last time you saw Chloe, ma'am?"

"'Ma'am?'" Aggy asked.

"Please stop interrupting my investigation, Aggy," Logan said, casting her a sharp look. He turned back to Kian's mom. "Ma'am?"

"I guess it was before dinner last night," she said. "I always put her out before we eat."

"You put her in the yard, ma'am?"

"Yes."

"Is the yard fenced, ma'am?"

"Yes."

"Is it secure, ma'am?"

"I guess."

"You guess, ma'am? You're not sure? It's possible Chloe could have gotten out on her own?"

"I suppose. . . ."

"Do you mind if we inspect the yard, ma'am?"

"We don't need permission to go into my own backyard, Logan," Kian said.

He led them through the kitchen and out the back door.

"Fan out and look for possible escape routes," Logan said.

"Sure thing, captain," Kian said.

They fanned out, but before long Kian and Thatcher were tussling in the grass again.

"This fence is pretty low, ma'am," Logan said to Kian's mom.

"Chloe's pretty low," she replied.

"What I mean, ma'am, is somebody could have easily reached over this fence and abducted your pet."

"I suppose they could have. But she's pretty noisy, especially when strangers go by the house."

"That's true," Thatcher piped in from across the yard, where he was sitting on Kian's back. "She always barks like crazy at me."

"What are you trying to do?" Kian grunted. "Hatch me?"

"Yeah! I'm Hatcher! Get it? Not Thatcher. *Hatcher!*"

"That's very funny," Kian said, without meaning it. "Can you please get off me, large boy?"

Logan ignored them. "Did you happen to hear

any barking last night during dinner, ma'am?" he asked Kian's mom.

She glanced upward, trying to recall. "I don't remember her barking. But she barks so much, I don't know if I'd have noticed."

"How about you, Kian?" Logan asked.

"I don't know," Kian grunted. "I forgot to keep a record of her barking habits last night, Logan. Sorry."

Logan wrote more notes on his chart.

"Will you boys stop that roughhousing before someone gets hurt?" Kian's mom asked.

"We're outside, Mom," Kian said. "We're roughyarding." He twisted and Thatcher toppled onto the grass.

"There aren't any escape routes back here, ma'am," Logan said to Kian's mom with a grim expression. "I'm sorry to inform you of this, but Chloe has been abducted by aliens. Don't worry, though. The Intergalactic Canine Rescue Unit is on the case."

"The what?" Kian's mom asked.

"The Intergalactic Canine Rescue Unit, ma'am. The ICRU. We'll get Chloe back."

Thatcher heard this and jumped to his feet. He flipped his hair out of his eyes and said, "Oh, yeah! The ICRU. That's us. We are so on the job!"

7. Pickles

The next morning Logan woke up early again, ate his breakfast, packed his gear, and headed to Sandwiches to resume his surveillance. There was a light drizzle falling, though the sun was shining, a typical occurrence in April in Nelsonport.

A block before Logan reached the store, he spotted a flyer on a telephone pole. On it was a color image of the dog he was sure he'd seen abducted by aliens. Above the picture were the words LOST DOG.

Across the street, he saw another copy of the poster tacked to another telephone pole. And another down the street. Logan peeked left and right, then reached up, ripped the flyer from the pole, and stuffed it into his bag.

He removed it later at school, and smoothed it out on the table for his fellow operatives of the Intergalactic Canine Rescue Unit.

"That's the dog," he said.

"The one that vanished?" Thatcher asked. "The one you saw from the bus?"

Aggy looked up from her book and said, "Hmm. You sure this is the dog, Logan?"

"That's the dog," he answered.

"Maybe she was taken after all," Aggy said, studying the poster carefully. "Her name is Pickles. Looks like some sort of spaniel mix."

"Pickles?" Thatcher asked. "A dog called Pickles? Who calls a dog 'Pickles'?"

"Trudy does," Aggy said, pointing at the woman's name.

"Let's call her and tell her an alien took her dog," Kian said with a straight face.

"Yeah!" Thatcher said.

Aggy looked up at them. "It wasn't an alien."

"Yes, it was," Logan said. "I have a sense about these things."

"And how many times has that sense of yours been correct?" Aggy asked.

"Nineteen," Logan said. "I've just never appre-hended one, that's all. They're not easy to catch. You ever caught an alien, Aggy?"

"Nope."

"I haven't, either," Kian deadpanned.

"That's because they're not easy to catch," Logan said.

"Not easy to throw, either, I bet," Kian said, and threw his pencil at Thatcher. It bounced off his chest.

"Ow!" Thatcher said, and cocked his fist to reciprocate when Nathan appeared at their table.

"How's the astronomy project going, guys?" he asked.

"Good, Nathan," Kian said.

"We're going to put on a skit," Thatcher said. "I'm going to be a meteorite."

"Not a black hole?" Kian asked.

Thatcher kicked him under the table, and said, "Kian's going to be a dwarf star."

Kian stared daggers at Thatcher. He didn't like cracks about his height.

"Sounds good," Nathan said. "What about you, Logan?"

"I'll be portraying an organism of superior intelligence from a faraway galaxy hurtling through space in a spacecraft made entirely of ice," Logan said.

"I come along and smash into him and turn his ship into ice cubes," Thatcher said.

"Not crushed ice?" Kian said.

"Better!" Thatcher said.

"Actually, no," Logan said. "The alien destroys the meteorite with a cryogenic torpedo."

"No way," Thatcher said. "I dodge that."

"Okay, some good ideas," Nathan said. "But get them down on paper, too. You should be making costumes and rehearsing by now."

"Costumes?" Thatcher asked. "We have to make costumes?"

"Produce!" Nathan said, and walked away.

"Who cares about a stupid skit," Logan said. "We have more important work to do."

"I'll help you find the dognapper," Aggy said.

"Yes!" Thatcher said, pumping his fist. "The ICRU to the rescue!"

"I don't like the 'Intergalactic' part," Aggy said. "Can't we just call it the CRU?"

"I created this task force," Logan said, "and I say it's the *Intergalactic* Canine Rescue Unit. The I-Crew, if you like."

"I won't be involved, then," Aggy said, opening her book. "And I'm the only one with a cell phone."

Logan scowled at her. "Okay," he said. "The CRU."

"Yeah!" Thatcher said, doing a little hip-swiveling dance in his chair. "The *Crew*!"

8. Yes, Ma'am

After class, the boys of the CRU huddled in the parking lot around Aggy as she switched the call with Trudy to speakerphone.

"My name is Aggy, and I'm calling about your lost dog."

"Oh, have you seen her?" the woman asked eagerly. "Did you find her?"

"No," Aggy said, "but my friend might have been nearby when she disappeared."

"Vanished," Logan whispered.

Aggy glared at him.

"In front of Sandwiches?" the woman asked.

"Yes."

"Did your friend see someone take her? You see, her collar and leash were left behind, which was strange. . . ."

"My friend didn't see anyone. I'm sorry."

"Tell her about the hairy man," Logan said, reaching for the phone. "Let me talk to her."

Aggy pressed it to her chest. "Shut it or I hang up."

Logan stepped back, scowling.

"My friend did see a man petting Pickles before she disappeared," Aggy said into the phone. "A man with a bushy beard."

"That's funny," Trudy said. "I met a man with a beard in the store that day."

"Ask her if he had an accent," Logan said loud enough for the lady to hear.

"Yes, he did," Trudy answered. "Who said that? Is that your friend?"

"Yes," Aggy said with a sigh. "That's Logan."

"Hello, ma'am," Logan said, moving closer to the phone.

"The man with the beard did have an accent," Trudy said.

"And then he went into the store, ma'am?" Logan asked.

"Will you knock it off with the 'ma'am'?" Aggy said.

"I like it," Trudy said. "It's polite. Respectful. Not too many young people these days are polite and respectful."

Logan stuck his tongue out at Aggy.

"Before he spoke to me," Trudy went on, "the man asked another woman if it was her dog tied up outside. I told him Pickles was mine."

"So he was looking for the dog's owner?" Logan asked.

"Yes. I don't know why. But he said Pickles was adorable and asked me her name."

"Did you tell him?" Logan asked.

"I did," Trudy said. "Shouldn't I have?"

Aggy shot Logan a reproachful look for worrying the woman, then spoke into the phone. "Of course you should have."

"He said, 'Pickles? Like the cucumber treat?' Then he laughed," Trudy said. "I guess he thought it was a funny name. I don't think so. My grandmother's name was Pickles."

"A woman named Pickles?" Kian whispered to Thatcher.

"Be nice," Thatcher said, then punched him in the stomach. Kian fired a punch back, but missed.

"I guess it's not so common anymore," Trudy said. "My grandmother was born in 1891."

"Whoa," Thatcher said. "Trudy must be *old*."

"If we see Pickles, we'll let you know," Aggy said into the phone. "I hope you find her."

"Oh, I do, too," said Trudy sadly. "She's only my best friend in the whole world, especially since my husband died."

"Aww," Thatcher said. "Poor old lady."

"Aww," Kian mocked, then landed a knuckle thump to Thatcher's sternum that knocked his breath away.

When he could talk again, Thatcher said, "That was cold, dude!" and struck back.

"Be quiet!" Logan commanded.

"How many children are there with you, Aggy?" Trudy asked.

"There are three little boys here with me, Trudy," Aggy answered, looking at them in disgust.

She and Trudy then traded good-byes, and Aggy closed her phone.

"You guys are apes," she said.

"Speaking of which, we must find the hairy

guy," Logan said. "We have to find him now, before he takes any more dogs."

"You have no evidence at all that he took Pickles," Aggy said. "Or Chloe."

"He went inside to find out the dog's name."

"That makes him a dognapper? Did you even see him come out?"

Logan sighed. "No."

"So he was still in the store when you got on the bus?" Aggy asked.

"I guess."

"So how did he steal Pickles?"

Logan just looked at her, waiting.

"Oh, I get it," Aggy said. "He was an alien. He could do whatever he wanted."

Logan answered with a knowing tilt of his head.

"It's a hairy alien?" Thatcher said. "Can aliens be hairy? Are you thinking of Bigfoot?"

"Aliens are not all little green men," said Logan. "Or tall green men with big eyes. Most of them can change form. They can be whatever they want to be. They could make themselves look like you, even. To be an alien, you just need to come from another planet. If you went to another planet, you'd be an alien, Thatcher."

"Really?" Hair flip. "Cool."

"It should be noted that my mom didn't see any hairy guy with an accent when Chloe was stolen," Kian said.

"Exactly," Logan said. "She didn't *see* him. That doesn't mean he wasn't there."

"You call that logic?" Aggy asked.

"I call it deducing," Logan said. "Ever heard of it?"

"Will you guys stop arguing so we can go find this guy?" Thatcher asked. "Where do we look, Logan?"

"We split up. Aggy can stake out the library. Kian, take Ketchoklam Park. Thatcher, downtown. And I'll take Sandwiches."

"I can't hang out downtown," Thatcher said. "My mom doesn't let me. Not by myself."

"I was going to the library anyway," Aggy said.

"What about you, Kian?" Logan asked.

"Sure, I'll go to the park to look for the hairy alien," he said.

"I'll go with him," Thatcher said. "I'm allowed

to go to the park if I'm with a friend."

"Logan!" a voice interrupted. "What are you doing?"

Logan turned to see his mom striding toward him. She was dressed up and wearing makeup, which meant she'd been with a client.

"I've been waiting in the car for you," she said, out of breath. "I've got to get you to Patrice's house. I have a client in ten minutes. Sloane and Bubba are in the car. Move it!"

"But, Mom, the Crew has investigating to do."

"Sorry, guys," she said to the group, then grabbed Logan's hand and pulled him away.

He twisted around and yelled, "CRU, find the hairy man with the accent!"

"The Crew is so on it!" Thatcher said, flashing a thumbs-up.

"There goes our fearless leader." Aggy sighed. "Off to his babysitter's house."

9. The Housesitter

"Who are you?" Logan asked the man who answered the door.

"I'm Buck," the man answered. He was wearing black sweatpants, a pale orange sweatshirt, and green slippers. "Come in," he said, stepping aside.

Logan was nudged inside by his mom. She followed behind, holding Sloane in one arm.

"I'll leave Bubba out here on the porch," she said to Buck. "You'll be glad I did. She's flatulent."

"Oh," said Buck.

"Where's Patrice?" Logan asked.

"Logan, this is Patrice's friend, Buck," his mom explained. "Remember, I told you Patrice is out of town? Buck is watching her house. I've known Buck a long time. He's going to watch you and

41

Sloane today." She set Sloane down and kissed him on the head.

"Hi, Sloane and Logan," Buck said, waving his arm like a windshield wiper.

Logan sneered.

"I have to run," his mom said, heading out the door. "Be good, guys. Have fun."

She waved at Logan as she flew down the steps, then climbed into her car and sped away.

"I suppose you know where everything is," Buck said to Logan.

"I've only been coming here since before I can remember," Logan said.

"I guess that means you know."

"I know."

Sloane began to whimper.

"He's probably upset because you're not Patrice," Logan said.

"You might be right, Logan," Buck said, and crouched down beside Sloane. "You want to go outside and swing?"

Sloane stopped whimpering.

"I'll push him," Logan said. "Sloane likes it

best when Patrice pushes him, and he likes me to push him second best. He doesn't even know you."

"Good point," Buck said.

Logan led them outside to the tire swing in the backyard. Buck hoisted Sloane up into it.

"Move aside now," Logan said, and nudged Buck's hip with his shoulder.

"Uh . . . sure," Buck said, backing away.

Logan gave Sloane a hard push.

"Too high! Too high! *Patrice!*" Sloane wailed.

"It's not too high, and Patrice isn't here," Logan said, and pushed him again, just as hard.

"Patrice! Patrice!" Sloane wailed louder.

"Oh, forget it," Logan said, disgusted. "You can push him, Buck. Only don't push him too high."

"I'd be happy to," Buck said. He caught the high-swinging Sloane, then restarted him with a gentle push.

"Come on, Bubba," Logan said.

Bubba, who had found a spot she liked near a tree and fallen asleep, rose to her feet, one leg at a time, and followed Logan around to the front of the house. She chose another spot she liked and lay down again with a heavy sigh. *"Unnnh, unnnh, unnnh,"* she said.

Logan wondered whether the other Crew operatives had found the hairy man yet. He wished he had a cell phone so he could check in with them.

"Here I am," he said aloud to himself, "locked in an interplanetary battle for Earth's dogs, and with no way of communicating with my co-operatives."

Then he had an idea. He went into the house and found Patrice's cordless phone. He dialed Aggy's number.

"Hello, Logan," she answered. "How's the baby-sitter?"

"Patrice is my caregiver, not my babysitter, and she isn't here. Her housesitter, Buck, is watching us. Did you find the hairy guy yet?"

"No. It's only been, like, twenty minutes or something, hasn't it? And he could be anywhere."

"He's not at the library?"

"I've seen men with beards. I haven't heard any bearded man speak with an accent, but this is a library, and people don't talk very much."

"Curses!" Logan said. "Call me at this number if you find the guy. If I find him, I'll call you." And he hung up.

He started to head back outside, then changed his mind. "I better stay by the phone."

He sat on the couch under Patrice's bay window and took out his clipboard. He saw a group of middle-schoolers walking down the street, two boys and a girl. He saw the woman who lived across the street kneeling in her flowers, pulling weeds and tossing them into a wheelbarrow. He noticed a telephone pole papered with flyers. He pulled out his binoculars and focused on them. One said, in big, bold letters, MISSING DOG.

10. The Third Dog

Logan ran outside. Bubba stood up slowly.

"Sit, Bubba!" Logan ordered as he passed by. "Stay!"

Bubba sat. Bubba stayed.

Logan was not surprised to find that a couple of the flyers on the pole were about lost dogs. Others advertised garage sales, rooms for rent, and a motorcycle for sale. One reported the disappearance of an electric wheelchair. Logan ripped down the ones about the missing dogs.

"Hey, there!" a voice from behind him said. "What are you doing?"

Logan spun around and saw the weeding lady coming toward him. She had white hair, a wrinkly face, and glasses that magnified her eyes.

She held a small metal claw in her hand, and her knees were muddy.

"What are you doing there?" she asked.

"I'm not stealing, ma'am," Logan said. "I'm part of a team that is investigating dognappings in the area. . . ."

"One of those flyers is mine," the lady said, waving a finger at the flyers he'd pulled down.

"Which one?" Logan asked, fanning out the flyers.

She singled out a picture of a small Pomeranian mix. "That's my Ollie," she said sadly.

"Can you describe the circumstances, ma'am?" Logan asked, holding up his clipboard. "You can trust me. I'm the chief investigator of the ICRU." He knew they had dropped the *Intergalactic*, but while he was on his own, he included it.

"The what?" the woman asked.

"The Intergalactic Canine Rescue Unit, ma'am. When was the last time you saw your dog?"

"Yesterday," the lady said.

"And what happened?"

"Well, I was out here tending the flowers, and Ollie was running around, playing. Digging

47

and growling is what he likes doing most. Then I stopped hearing him, so I went to look for him."

"Had he vanished?" Logan asked.

"Completely," the lady said, her chin beginning to quiver. "All I found was his collar."

Logan looked up from his note-taking. "His collar, ma'am?"

"Yes. He must have pulled it off. He does that sometimes."

Logan wrote furiously.

"Why aren't you in school?" the lady asked. "Is it a holiday I don't know about?"

"No, ma'am," Logan said, still writing. "I attend an alternative education program, ma'am. I only go to school three times a week, and only for a couple hours at a time."

"It's a private school?"

"No, ma'am. NICE is part of the public school system."

"NICE?"

"It's an acronym for Nelsonport Individualized Choice Education."

"I see. . . ." the woman said, though she still appeared confused.

"Did you happen to see a stranger around that day, ma'am? A hairy man? A hairy man with an accent?"

The lady's brow furrowed as she considered this. "No. Not that I can remember, anyway. . . ."

"Think, ma'am!" Logan said, causing the woman to jump. "It's important. Very important. Did you or did you not see a hairy man with an accent on the day your dog vanished? He might have had dog treats on him."

"Logan?" Buck called before the flustered lady could answer. He was across the street, holding Sloane by the hand. "I need you to stay on the property, Logan."

Logan ignored him. "Did you, ma'am? Did you see a hairy man around here? Did you? Huh? Did you?"

"Logan?" Buck said. "Come on back now."

"I'm going to need these flyers to help you get your dog back, ma'am," Logan said to the lady. "You can print up another one, can't you?"

"Logan," Buck said. He and Sloane were now across the street.

"Goga!" Sloane said.

"I have to go, ma'am," Logan said. "But I'll be back. Don't worry about anything, ma'am. We'll find your dog."

"We?" she asked.

"The ICRU, ma'am."

"Oh, yes," the woman said.

Logan walked to where Buck and Sloane were standing, but did not stop.

Buck followed after him. "What were you talking to her about?" he asked.

Logan didn't answer. He marched straight up to Bubba.

"Come on, girl," he said. "I'm taking you into the house even if you do fart. It's for your own protection. I don't want some hairy alien with an accent dognapping you."

Bubba climbed to her feet again and followed Logan inside. She sat at Logan's feet as Logan punched Aggy's number, and whimpered, "*Unnnh, unnnh, unnnh.*"

The call went to voice mail.

After the beep, Logan said, "At least three dogs are missing in Patrice's neighborhood. One owner said her dog's collar was found in the yard. The alien—or aliens—have struck again. Let's rendezvous at Ketchoklam Park at two o'clock to discuss strategies. This is Logan, signing out."

And he hung up.

11. Crew Rendezvous

Ketchoklam was a lush, sloping city park perched high on a cliff overlooking the bay. Squids, sharks, whales, seals, and dolphins swam in the waters beyond the park. Enormous ships from Asia sailed by, completing their long Pacific voyages. Steel-gray nuclear submarines and aircraft carriers occasionally drifted past. At the base of the cliff was a rocky beach teeming with mussels and squawking gulls. In the distance stood towering snow-peaked Canadian volcanoes. Without much notice of any of this—they had gotten used to it—the Crew gathered on a wooden picnic table to compare notes.

Logan wasn't the only one who had brought missing-dog flyers. Kian had found two as well. And Aggy had torn down a few from telephone poles around the library.

Thatcher had seen lost-dog flyers, too, but had left them alone.

"I didn't think it was right to tear them down," he said. "What if someone saw the missing dogs, but there wasn't a flyer to tell them who to call? What would they do then? Huh?"

"No one's going to find these missing dogs, Thatcher," Logan said seriously. "These dogs are no longer on Earth, if they're alive at all. Who knows what the aliens want them for? Maybe they're using them for food, or for fuel for their spaceship. . . ."

"Gross," Aggy said.

"I bet the aliens just like dogs," Thatcher said. "Maybe they don't have any on their planet."

"Yes, I'm sure they traveled light-years for pets," Kian said. He then growled like a dog and jumped Thatcher.

"Cut it out, men," Logan said. "We have a lot of work to do."

"Like what?" Aggy asked. "Call the people on the flyers and ask them if they've seen the hairy man?"

"We don't have time for more interrogations,"

Logan said. "We need to find him ourselves before he takes any more dogs."

"You haven't established that this man was anywhere near any of the other dogs that were stolen," Aggy said. "You saw him pet a dog once. Big deal."

"I know an alien when I see one."

"Yeah, you were right about that sub we had last month," Aggy said.

"I'm telling you, that guy wasn't human," Logan said. "He had antennae coming out of his head."

"Really?" said Thatcher. "He had antennae? Like a bug?"

"I saw them."

"Yeah," Kian said. "Lots of substitutes have antennae."

"How are we going to find the hairy guy?" Aggy asked.

"We're going to use one of our dogs for bait," Logan said, eyeing each of them.

"I'm not letting Bear be bait," Thatcher said. "No way. I don't want some alien to zap him."

Logan looked at Kian.

"Chloe's unavailable," he said. "Remember?"

"Don't you have another dog?" Logan asked.

"My dad has a cat," Kian said, with visible distaste.

"Like an alien would take a cat." Thatcher laughed.

Kian screamed like a leopard and bared pretend claws at Thatcher. Thatcher screamed and clawed back, and the two predators went at each other.

Logan looked to Aggy.

"Nope," she said. "Leave Festus out of it."

"I thought you weren't afraid of aliens?" Logan said.

"I'm not. Festus just had surgery and needs to rest."

"Oh, all right. We can use Bubba," Logan said. "I'll go get her and bring her to Sandwiches. We'll all meet there."

"I can't go to Sandwiches," Thatcher said. "I've got soccer."

"Me, too," said Aggy.

"I have piano," Kian said.

"Yeah, Kian has piano lessons," Thatcher said

in a lilting, teasing voice, while pretending to tap piano keys on Kian's head.

Kian punched him in the gut, which prompted a slugfest.

"Silence!" Logan shouted.

The fighting stopped. Everyone stared at him.

"We are in the midst of an alien invasion, people," he said. "I don't want to hear about your other commitments."

"Logan!" a voice called out. "Logan! What are you doing here?" His mom was running toward him, Sloane in her arms, his head bobbing.

His shoulders slumped. "Not *again*."

"I guess we won't be trapping any aliens today after all," Aggy said.

"Buck said you just walked away without telling him where you were going," his mom said.

"I had to, Mom," Logan said. "It was vital."

His mom stopped in front of him, caught her breath, and said, "Move it, bud. Into the car. I'm mad. You're in trouble. Move it."

"But Mom—"

"Nope," she said, shifting Sloane into one arm and taking Logan's hand. "Sorry, Crew, but I need your leader!" she called over her shoulder as she pulled him away.

"That's okay, Jenny," Kian said, waving at them. "Bye."

They all stood silent for a moment, then headed off toward their scheduled activities.

12. The Fate of the World's Dogs

"Son, you do not walk away from the person I have given authority to take care of you," Logan's mom said.

Logan was pinned in an easy chair in the living room, his mom leaning over him. He knew never to speak when his mother's face was red. At the moment, it was like a huge strawberry.

"Okay?" she asked.

He nodded. Nodding was usually okay.

She relaxed and sank into the couch. "Was this about the aliens taking the dogs?"

Logan nodded again.

His mom straightened her spine and folded her legs into the lotus position. She rested her hands on her knees, palms up, closed her eyes, and breathed mindfully. That was what she called it: mindful breathing. Deep inhalation. Hold it. Long, slow, audible exhalation. And again. The red began to pale.

Sloane sat beside her and did his best to imitate her.

"I saw signs," Logan said softly. "Across the street. Lost-dog signs. I had to investigate. I met a lady whose dog vanished."

His mom stopped her mindful breathing. "Lots of people's dogs 'vanish,' Logan."

"But Ollie vanished like Pickles did, Mom. The alien zapped him right out of his collar. His owner found it in the grass."

"Really?" his mom asked.

"Pickles," Sloane said. "I want pickles."

"Not now, Sloane," his mom said.

"Dogs are vanishing all over town, Mom. And there's this strange man with lots of hair and an accent."

"Are the aliens French hippies or something?"

"The hair isn't just on their heads, Mom. It's on their necks and hands, too."

"Could be Sasquatch."

"You're making fun of me."

"Sorry. How about I send out a mass e-mail to everyone I know. I'll even send one to my clients in the FBI. Okay?"

Logan wasn't sure if he could trust her. She sometimes promised to do things she knew he could not verify.

"Do it now," Logan said. "I want to watch you do it."

"Oh, not now, Logan. I'm tired. And I have a million things to do. . . ."

"Mom," Logan said, standing up. "You are not getting this. We are in the midst of an alien invasion. That's why I left Patrice's. This is an *emergency*. Me and the Crew were going to set a trap for the aliens when you came and dragged me home. We have important work to do. We must stop these extraterrestrial dognappers from taking our dogs!"

His mom snickered.

"It's not funny!" Logan hollered at her, then stomped away.

"It was the 'extraterrestrial dognappers' that got me, son," she called after him. "I'm sorry."

Logan scooped up the phone as he walked by it, then went into his room and slammed the door.

"No door slamming!" his mom yelled.

"Slam!" echoed Sloane.

Logan looked out his window. Bubba was lying on the back patio. The backyard was fenced in, though it wasn't necessary anymore. When Bubba was younger she might have run off, but now she was too old.

Logan slid his bedroom window open and popped out the screen.

13. Alien Bait

Bubba spread out on the damp sidewalk outside Sandwiches. Logan had tied her to the bike rack. He knew he didn't need to but he wanted to set the stage the same way it had been with Pickles.

"Be a good girl," he said to his dog, and hugged her saggy neck tightly, just in case the aliens did zap her and he never saw her again.

"Unnnh, unnnh, unnnh," she said.

Logan let go of her, scratched her head, said, "Try not to fart," then crossed the street to his observation post.

He put on his binoculars, camera, and sunglasses, then got out his clipboard. He couldn't read his watch through the dark glasses so he took them off and set them on the branch of the dogwood tree.

"Don't forget them this time," he said to himself.

He recorded the time, location, and weather conditions: 3:53, Sandwiches, light drizzle. He then brought his binoculars up to his eyes, and watched.

Regular school was out, so kids were getting off buses and going into the store and coming out with bags of chips and sodas. Some sat around on benches talking and texting and snacking; some wandered over to the library; some stopped to pet Bubba. A few of them stood up quickly, fanned their hands in front of their faces, and hurried away.

Logan recorded it all. His dog's life, and the lives of all the other dogs of Nelsonport, depended on his being vigilant.

"I will not falter," he said to himself. "It is my destiny to thwart the aliens' fiendish plot."

"What're you doing there, guy?" a boy said, walking up.

Logan glanced at him. He guessed the boy was about thirteen. He was with two other kids who looked to be the same age. One was a girl, the other a boy. The boy was gripping the girl's hand.

"You spying on somebody?" this boy asked.

"Are you a spy, guy?" asked the other boy.

Logan recognized that they were getting ready to have some fun at his expense.

"Take a hike," he said, pointing with his thumb in the direction he wanted them to go.

The boys laughed.

The girl said, "Leave him alone, Burke. Let's go."

Burke stepped closer to Logan.

"Trust me," Logan said without looking at him. "You don't want to get involved in this."

"Really?" Burke said. "It's dangerous work? Dangerous spy work? Something one needs a clipboard for?"

He let his girlfriend's hand drop and snatched Logan's clipboard.

Logan whirled on him.

"Give it back!" he yelled. "Give it back, you idiot!"

The boy danced away, laughing.

"Give it back to him, Burke," the girl said.

Logan kept lunging and grasping and scream-
ing at the boy to give it back, but Burke just tossed
it to the other boy.

"Stop it, Burke," the girl said.

She approached the second boy.

"Give it to me, Wyndham."

He slumped his shoulders and handed it over.

"Aw, dude," Burke groaned.

She handed it to Logan, who snatched it from
her.

"You idiots don't know what you're doing," he
said. "You don't understand what's at stake."

He resumed his observation post and returned
his attention to Bubba.

Who wasn't there.

"Bubba!" he screamed. "Bubba!"

Logan tossed away the clipboard and bolted
toward Sandwiches. Along the way he flung off
the camera and binoculars.

"Bubba!" he kept yelling. "Bubba!"

"What a freak!" Burke laughed, and gave
Wyndham a high five.

"What a loser," his girlfriend said, shaking her
head and picking up the clipboard.

14. Maybe It's Moms

Bubba's collar and leash had not been left behind. They had disappeared with her.

"Over here, Logan," a voice called out.

His mom sat at the end of one of the several long wooden benches in front of the store, petting Bubba.

"Mom!" Logan said, stomping to her. "What are you doing here? I thought the aliens got Bubba!"

"Nope," his mom said. "No aliens. Just Mom. By any chance did you climb out your window again and leave without getting permission from, or even notifying, your parental unit?"

"I *had* to, Mom. Someone has to do something. Someone has to stop the aliens from stealing our dogs."

"Maybe it isn't aliens. Maybe it's moms. Maybe

their sons keep leaving their dogs all alone outside grocery stores and the moms have to come and rescue them." She smiled wide and blinked. She had amused herself.

"Excuse me," a voice said. "Here's your stuff."

It was the girl who had been with Burke and Wyndham. She handed Logan his clipboard and his binoculars and camera, which she had also scooped up. Logan took them without a word.

"Thank you, considerate young lady," his mom said. "I'm sure my son is grateful, too, but he's too tongue-tied by your beauty to say so."

Logan kicked her.

"Ow!" she howled exaggeratedly. "Now that's parent abuse!"

"I'm sorry Burke was so mean to you," the girl said with a tiny shrug. Then she walked away.

"Who's Burke?" Logan's mom asked.

"It doesn't matter," Logan said. "I was using Bubba to attract the aliens, Mom. That's why I left her alone. I was across the street watching."

"Not very well, I guess, since you thought aliens took her instead of your dear, sweet mother."

"I got . . . distracted."

"By Burke?"

"It doesn't matter!" Logan said, then stomped away.

He didn't like being deterred from his duties by either bored, malicious teenagers or his meddlesome mother. He also hated it when his mom joked around when things were deadly serious.

He stopped stomping when he reached the end of the building. An old man with a humped back was sitting in a wheelchair, reading a newspaper. The wheelchair had a motor under the seat, white rubber tires, padded seat and armrests, and a joystick for steering. Logan wished he had one like it.

Then he remembered the MISSING WHEELCHAIR flyer he saw on the telephone pole across the street from Patrice's house. This old guy's chair looked a lot like the one in the flyer. Had he stolen it?

No, he was an old guy who needed a wheel-chair. How could he steal one?

The man peeked out from behind his paper,

as if sensing someone staring at him. Though he immediately ducked back behind it when he saw Logan standing there, Logan noted some details: the man wore a dark blue stocking cap pulled down low, a pair of huge, dark, old-people sunglasses, and stubbly gray whiskers on his chin and cheeks. Logan pulled out his clipboard and jotted all this down.

"Logan," his mom called. "Come back and sit with me."

Logan continued writing.

"Logan?" his mom said.

He turned. "What?"

"Come here," she said.

He stomped back toward her, stopping a couple of yards away.

"What?" he said again.

"Sit down, please," she said, patting the seat beside her.

"I don't want to."

"You're having a hard time doing what I ask lately, aren't you, bud?"

He wrinkled his nose at her like an annoyed cat.

"I'll let you return to your surveillance. I'll even let you use Bubba as alien bait. But I don't want you running away without permission, from me or from others I've asked to care for you. Buck, for example."

"Buck!" Logan said, rolling his eyes.

His mom stood.

"I'll leave you to your work, Crewman Lonergan."

"Crew *captain*," he said, and grinned at the thought of it.

"But if you climb out your window again, I will ground you for a week. Let's see you foil a full-scale alien invasion from your bedroom."

"Deal," Logan said, and stepped forward to shake on it.

"Okay then," his mom said, taking his hand. "Back to your post."

15. The Fourth Dog

After his mom had gone, Logan retied Bubba to the bike rack and returned to the dogwood tree on the library's lawn. His sunglasses were on the branch, blanketed in a film of mist. He wiped them on his jeans, slipped them into his backpack, and, to prevent his forgetting them again, decided he would leave them there. He rehung his binoculars and camera around his neck, then, clipboard poised, turned his attention to Bubba.

Sandwiches always bustled after school let out. Logan had a full-time job recording all the activity: the two gray-haired, power-walking ladies who stopped and petted Bubba; the trio of boys who parked their bikes by her, then waved away the hovering odor; swarms of teenagers, some of whom paid attention to Bubba, some who were too into their own world to notice her; the men (many of them bearded) and sometimes women wearing dirty work clothes who pulled up in trucks, went into the store, and came out with a beverage of some kind; the ruddy-faced sailors, male and female, young and old, striding in knee-high rubber waders; the moms, and sometimes dads, pushing strollers, or toting their child in carriers on their backs, chests, or hips; the old guy in the wheelchair parked at the end of the bench, his face hidden behind his newspaper; and, of course, plenty of people walking dogs. Some walked two, some three. One walker had a large, a medium, and a small: a Newfie, a spaniel, and a wiener dog. The walkers tied their dogs up, or just left them, untied, and went into the store. Some of the dogs growled at Bubba, but she never growled back, or even budged, so they eventually left her alone.

Logan paid special attention to keeping track of the dogs, making sure the ones left outside got picked up, and by their rightful owners, not by someone else.

No dogs vanished. The hairy man with the

accent did not appear. Nothing unusual or suspicious happened, which Logan found almost disappointing. He didn't want anyone's dog abducted, especially not Bubba, but he had been hoping *something* would happen—a dognapping attempt, maybe, that he would sweep in and foil. The alien would then be unveiled, apprehended, arrested, and everyone would learn he had been right all along.

No such luck.

After nearly an hour of surveillance, Logan began to get hungry. His eyes hurt from squinting through his binoculars. The cords of the binoculars and the camera had dug a trench into the back of his neck. He decided to pack up and call it a day.

As he walked over the lawn, he saw Aggy appear across the street with her dog, Festus, a fat, sausage-shaped beagle/dachshund mix with a black-and-white coat and stubby legs. From a distance, he looked like a miniature cow.

"Aggy!" Logan called, but she didn't hear him over a noisy delivery truck coming up the street. She bent over and petted Bubba, then stood up, her face puckered, and waved her hand in front of her nose.

The truck pulled up to the curb, obscuring her and the dogs. Logan ran across the street and around the front of the truck. He nearly collided with the old man in the electric wheelchair, who was zooming past.

"Excuse me," the man said.

Logan didn't answer. He was too busy looking for Aggy. He didn't see her. She must have gone into the store. Bubba, still tied to the bike rack, was on her feet, whimpering, as if frightened.

"It's okay," Logan said, rubbing Bubba's head. "I'm watching out for you. Where's Festus?"

That's when he noticed a collar lying beside Bubba on the sidewalk. It was attached to a retractable leash, and buckled, as if it were still around a dog's neck. The collar was made of faded pink nylon with white polka dots. Logan knew it instantly.

"Not again," he said, swiveling his head left and right, like an owl looking for prey. A few people sat on the benches, chatting, snacking, sipping. A woman was tucking her baby into a stroller. The old man's wheelchair was humming as it navigated the crosswalk. A kid rode up on her skateboard. Logan looked at Bubba.

"Where's Festus?" he asked.

"Unnnh, unnnh, unnnh," Bubba said.

Logan darted into the store, yelling, "Aggy! Aggy!"

The cashiers and customers at the check-out counters stopped what they were doing and stared.

"Have you seen Aggy?" he asked them. "It's urgent."

"There's a girl over—" one of the cashiers began to say, when Aggy appeared at the end of an aisle.

"Logan!" she said, her jaw tight. "What are you yelling about?"

Logan rushed to her. "Where's Festus?"

"Outside," Aggy said.

"No, he's not."

"I tied him next to Bubba. I thought you'd be in here. . . ."

"He's not tied next to Bubba. Come on. I'll show you."

He took her arm and tugged.

"Let go!" she said, and jerked her arm free.

"It's just his collar and leash. Like before. With Pickles. Come see."

"What?" Aggy said, her resistance evaporating. "Just his collar?"

"Pink with white polka dots," Logan said.

Aggy raced for the door.

16. After the Hairy Guy

"The alien vaporized him right out of his collar," Logan said.

"Maybe he slipped out of it somehow," Aggy said hopefully. "You know. Squeezed out of it. To get free."

"Not likely," Logan said.

Festus, like Bubba, was a slow-moving, older dog. He'd also recently undergone hip surgery. He wasn't prone to escape attempts.

"Maybe somebody undid his collar," Aggy said. "Then rebuckled it. You know, for a joke. A prank."

"I've been casing the corner for hours," Logan said. "I saw everybody who came and went and wrote down everything they did. I ran over when I saw you, but a truck pulled up and blocked my vision. You know, it must have happened right then. Shoot! If it weren't for that stupid truck, I would have witnessed the dognapping!"

"How could somebody have unbuckled him, taken him, and rebuckled the collar that fast?" Aggy asked.

"That's just it. No human could have. Did you talk to anyone? Did anyone ask what your dog's name was?"

"Yeah, some lady did. She stopped and petted Festus and talked baby talk to him. Why?"

"What did she look like?"

"I don't know. She was an old lady. Gray hair. Short. I think she was wearing glasses. And tennis shoes . . ."

"Hmmm," Logan said, as he dug out his clipboard. "The hairy guy petted Pickles, then went into the store to look for her owner. He asked Trudy what her dog's name was, then Pickles just disappeared. Without anyone around."

"But that didn't happen to Chloe. Or Ollie. They just disappeared."

"They were in their yards, unsupervised," Logan said. "We don't know who was around. Maybe the aliens take human form, then hang around a dog, listening, waiting to hear the dog's name. Maybe they need the dog's name to beam it."

"That's a lot of maybes."

"It's a theory," Logan said.

"I better call my mom and tell her Festus got away," Aggy said, pulling out her phone.

"You should call nine-one-one and inform the police your dog was abducted by aliens."

"Yeah, I'm not going to do that," Aggy said, pressing numbers, then putting the phone to her ear. "Hi, Mom. Can you meet me at Sandwiches? Festus—"

Aggy stopped midsentence because a man pushed open the door beside her and exited the store, a plastic bag of groceries in each hand. In each hairy hand. His face and neck were hairy, too.

"It's him!" Logan said. "It's the hairy man! The dognapper! The *alien*!"

"Shhh!" Aggy said, and elbowed Logan hard. "You're talking out loud, you know."

Logan hastened after the man and asked, "Excuse me, sir, but are you an alien?"

"Logan!" Aggy said.

The man's gait faltered. "What did you say?" he asked, looking over his shoulder at Logan, perplexed.

Logan took advantage of the man's disorientation to catch up with him.

"You have an accent, sir," Logan said. "You're an alien, are you not?"

"I don't know why you are saying this," the man said, walking faster, trying to get away from Logan. "It is nothing to you. Leave me alone."

Logan persisted. "Have you been abducting dogs, sir? Can you make dogs vanish? Do you need to know their name in order to do it?"

The man looked back, alarmed, then doubled his step. He was walking as fast as he could without breaking into a run.

"Leave him alone!" Aggy called, snapping her phone shut.

"We can't let him get away!" Logan called back. "Come on! We must follow him!"

"What about Bubba?" Aggy asked.

Logan skidded to a stop. He turned and yelled, "You said her name!"

"You can't just leave her here," Aggy said.

"Can you watch her?" Logan said, then shook his head, as if answering his own question. He ran back to his dog.

"I'll bring her with me," he grumbled, untying her from the bike rack.

"Why didn't the dognapper take her, too?" Aggy asked.

"Maybe because she farts so much," Logan said.

"I wish Festus did," Aggy said with a frown.

17. The Planet Crete

Logan tried to shadow the hairy man, but Bubba hampered his stealth considerably. It wasn't easy ducking behind trees or bushes with a large, lazy bloodhound tethered to him.

When the man disappeared around a hedge-lined corner, Logan thought he might take a diagonal shortcut. He managed to penetrate the dense hedge, but getting Bubba through it proved much more difficult. By the time he had extracted her, he assumed the hairy man had gotten away. However, after he and Bubba had loped across the yard and he had burrowed through the second hedge, Logan was startled to find the hairy man standing there, waiting for him.

"What are you doing, boy?" he asked, his fists

on his hips, his bushy eyebrows knitted together. "Why do you follow me?"

Bubba was still on the other side of the hedge. Logan decided she was safer there and dropped his end of the leash. He got to his feet and brushed the leaves and twigs from his clothes. He didn't know about the ones in his hair.

"Why are you abducting our dogs?" Logan asked, jutting his chin defiantly.

"I am *not* abducting dogs," the man said. "Why do you say such a thing?"

"Because you are an alien, of course," Logan said.

"That is none of your business, young man, and you are very rude to say it."

"Where did you come from?" Logan asked.

"If you must know, I am from Crete."

"What galaxy is that in?"

"Galaxy? Crete is in the Mediterranean."

"So there is a galaxy named after the sea. I did not know that. . . ."

"I am walking away now, young man, and I do not wish you should follow me, okay? Leave me alone now."

He turned and walked away, checking over his shoulder from time to time to see if Logan was behind him.

Logan didn't follow, because when he reached down for Bubba's leash, it wasn't there.

"Bubba?" he called, peering into the foliage. "Where are you?"

"Unnnh, unnnh, unnnh," his dog said.

She had walked away from the hedge, dragging her leash behind her, and found a spot she liked on the lawn.

"Bubba, *come*." Logan commanded.

She didn't budge.

"The alien is getting away!" Logan said.

He had no choice but to return through the hedge and collect his dog.

"What are you doing, Bubba?" he asked as he walked up to her, again shaking off twigs and leaves.

He scooped up Bubba's leash and led her out of the yard, this time taking the path from the house's front door. He wondered why he hadn't done so before.

Back on the street, he heard a voice call, "Hey, Logan!"

Without noticing it, Logan had ended up across the street from Thatcher's house, and Thatcher was on his way over.

"Where are you going?" he asked Logan.

"Perfect timing, Thatcher. The hairy man is trying to get away. He just abducted Festus."

"Aggy's dog? Where? How?"

"He zapped him right out of his collar. Come on. Let's find him."

"Uh, I need to tell my mom if I'm leaving," Thatcher said sheepishly.

"Fine," Logan said. "Hurry up. And do me a favor and leave Bubba at your house." He handed Thatcher Bubba's leash.

"Okay. I'll catch up to you. Come on, Bubba."

"Unnnh, unnnh, unnnh," Bubba said.

Thatcher put her in his backyard with his dog, Bear.

"Be nice to her, Bear," he said. "She's old. And she farts. So look out."

Then he ran into the house to tell his mom he was going.

"Are you sure that guy's an alien?" he asked Logan when he caught up with him. "I see him walking his dog by my house all the time."

"He admitted he was an alien," Logan answered. "And look at him trying to escape. He's clearly our dognapper."

"There he is!" Thatcher said, pointing.

The man was a couple of blocks ahead, crossing midblock.

"See?" Logan said. "He's jaywalking. He obviously does not respect our laws."

"I do it all the time," Thatcher said.

"But he's an adult," Logan said. "Come on!"

18. The Alien's Son

"Where'd he go?" Thatcher asked. The hairy man had disappeared. "Have you seen him? Are we in danger?"

"He must have beamed himself up to his ship," Logan said at last.

"If he could do that, why didn't he do it before?" Thatcher asked. "Why did he run away? If I could beam myself up, I wouldn't bother running away. . . ."

"He didn't want us to see him do it," Logan said. "Let's ask that kid if he's seen him."

They approached a boy standing in front of a small, pale green house.

"Are you chasing my dad?" the boy asked.

"Your dad?" Thatcher asked. "The hairy guy with the accent is your dad?"

"He said some crazy boy was chasing him and accusing him of stealing dogs."

"Is this your house?" Logan asked.

"No," the boy said. "But me and my family live in it."

"You live in a house that isn't yours?"

"We rent it."

"I've seen this kid before," Thatcher whispered in Logan's ear. "Walking the same dog the hairy guy walks."

"He must be an alien, too, then," Logan whispered back.

"Is this a prank or something?" the boy asked. "My dad doesn't get American pranks."

"Isn't he American?" Thatcher asked. "What is he?"

"He's Cretan. He was born in Crete."

"The island by Greece?" Thatcher asked. "Where the minotaur lived? I love the minotaur!"

"Right," the boy said. "Most people don't know anything about Crete."

"I *love* the Greek myths," Thatcher said. "The minotaur's awesome."

"Yeah," the boy said with a curling smile.

"He's not from Crete, Thatcher," Logan said. "He's the son of an alien."

The hairy man stepped out the front door, holding a cell phone.

"I am going to call the police if you don't leave my property at once," he said, glaring at Logan.

"The police?" Thatcher gasped. "My mom wouldn't like it if I got arrested, Logan. Maybe we should go. . . ."

"Go ahead and call the police," Logan said to the man. "I think you're bluffing. You don't want the police here."

"I am really going to call," the man said. "You cannot harass me this way, boy."

"Logan!" a voice yelled from down the street.

They all looked. At the intersection, Logan's mom was poking her head out the window of her car.

"Mom!" Logan yelled back. "What are you doing here?"

She turned the car and sped toward them.

"Okay, here comes my mom," Logan said to the man. "Now you're in for it. My mom doesn't mess around. She's a life coach, and one of her clients works for the FBI."

"A life coach?" the man asked.

Logan's mom pulled her car to the curb and jumped out.

"What are you doing here?" she asked, rushing up to Logan and grasping his arm. "You were supposed to stay at Sandwiches. I've been scouring the neighborhood for you!"

"This is one of the aliens, mom," Logan said, indicating the man standing in the front door. "He made Festus disappear. Probably Pickles, too."

His mom looked at the man with a pained expression on her face.

"I am going to call the police!" he said, shaking his fist in the air. "Your boy is harassing me! He is crazy!"

"I'm so sorry," Logan's mom said, moving toward him, her hand extended, her face bright red and screwed up to show her regret.

"Mom!" Logan shrieked. "Don't!"

"I'm Jenny Lonergan," she said. "My son has aliens on the brain, I'm afraid."

The man reluctantly unclenched his hand and let Logan's mom shake it.

"He accused me of stealing dogs," he said.

"His friend's dog went missing recently," Logan's mom said.

"Two friends," Logan interrupted. "Festus just got abducted. . . ."

"He's been upset about it," his mom broke in.

"But he shouldn't go about accusing people," the man said.

"I know, I know. I'm so sorry. Really. I am *so* sorry." She turned to Logan. "Logan, would you please tell this nice man how sorry you are?"

"For what?" Logan said. "He admitted he's an alien."

"He's from Crete," the man's son said.

"Crete?" Logan's mom said. "How interesting! How long have you lived here?"

"A year," the man said. "But we lived in Wisconsin for eight years before that."

"And this is your son?" Logan's mom extended her hand to the boy.

"Yes," the man said. "This is my Darius."

"Hi, Darius," Logan's mom said. She shook his

hand, too. His lank black hair swept back and forth with the motion. "You must be about . . . ten?"

"Yes," he said.

"Logan is ten, too," she said.

"And a sixth," Logan added.

"And this is Thatcher," his mom said, presenting him with a wave of her arm. "You're all about the same age."

"Hi," said Thatcher with a little wave. "I'll be ten in July. I live around the corner."

"I've seen you," Darius said. "Hi."

There was a silent pause, then Logan's mom said, "Well! We're going to leave you in peace now, Mr. . . ."

"Sarris," the man said.

"Mr. Sarris. Once again, I am so sorry."

She moved over to Logan and began easing him toward the car. When he resisted, she took his hand and pulled him.

"But *Mom*!" he said.

"Let's leave these nice people alone, son. Come on. . . ."

"No! Let . . . me . . . go!"

"He is very stubborn," the man said.

"Tell me about it," Logan's mom said, with an affected laugh.

"He gets this from his father?"

"No," Logan's mom said. "From his mother."

19. Return of the Second Dog

"Chloe's back," Kian said as he took his seat at the table.

The Crew, who had been chattering about Mr. Sarris, the hairy alien, fell silent.

"She just showed up in the backyard this morning," Kian added, then folded his hands on the table and blinked twice.

"She's back?" Thatcher asked. "Wasn't she abducted by aliens? How did she escape?"

"I guess she was too clever for them," Kian said with a shrug.

"Maybe the aliens didn't like her yapping and returned her," Logan said.

"Hey, maybe they'll return Festus, too,"

Thatcher said. "Huh, Aggy? Maybe the aliens won't like him, either."

Aggy kept her eyes on the pages of her book. She was rereading *Ginger Pye*, the story of a puppy that is stolen.

"I'm glad you got your dog back," she said to Kian.

"Gee, thanks," Kian said.

"He never liked Chloe very much, Aggy," Thatcher said.

"We went to the animal shelter," Aggy said, still not looking up from her book.

"Oh, really?" Logan asked. "Did you see any of the missing dogs on the flyers there?"

"I wasn't really thinking about them," Aggy said. "I was looking for Festus."

"I should go over there with the posters and see if any of them are there," Logan said to himself.

"Don't you think if the owners of the lost dogs went to the trouble of making flyers, they would have checked the shelter?" Aggy asked. "It's the first thing we did."

Logan didn't answer. He was thinking.

"I saw a dog I really liked," Aggy said.

"You did?" Thatcher asked. "Boy or girl?"

"Boy," Aggy said. "His name is Smoky."

"So he's gray?"

"Black. He had Lab in him."

"Listen," Thatcher said, rubbing his hands together, "I had an idea for how we could get all the dogs back. We build a giant dog whistle, right? The kind we can't hear but dogs can? Then the dogs hear it, and they all come back!"

"Great idea," Kian said, nodding exaggeratedly. "I think we should start making it right away. We could chop down a tree and carve out the middle with our pocket knives."

"Oh, you're going to get it!" Thatcher said, and dove across the table at him.

"Gentlemen?" Nathan said in a deep voice.

Thatcher, who had ended up on the floor, bounced to his feet, and chirped, "Sorry, Nathan! I'm focusing. I'll produce, I'll produce. . . ."

20. Lair of the Dognappers

"I say we stake out the alien's house and follow him wherever he goes," Logan said after class. "He's bound to head to his ship sooner or later, then we storm in and rescue the dogs."

"He's not an alien," Thatcher said. "His son seemed cool."

"Cool?" Logan said. "*Cool?* Tell that to Trudy. Tell it to Aggy."

"Chloe's back," Aggy said. "Maybe Pickles is."

"Yeah," Thatcher said. "We should call Trudy."

"It's not our business," Aggy said. "I wouldn't want strangers calling me about Festus."

"We don't need to call anyone," Logan said. "All we need to do is follow the hairy guy to his ship and rescue the dogs. As the Crew leader, I say we go stake out his house."

"Who made you leader?" Aggy asked.

"I don't think we should," Thatcher said. "I don't think we should bother Mr. Sarris anymore. He's not an alien. He's just a guy."

"I'll go," Aggy said, closing her book.

Thatcher gawked at her.

"I'll go, too," Kian said. "I've never seen an alien's ship before."

"Okay then," Logan said. "Let's go."

He, Kian, and Aggy walked off.

"Oh, all right," Thatcher said. "I'm coming. But I'm telling you the guy's just a guy."

They stopped at Sandwiches on the way to see if any of the flyers had been rehung. They found posters with pictures of missing dogs, including Pickles, on several telephone poles. Logan tore down the few he didn't have.

"You shouldn't take those down," Thatcher said.

"They can put up as many flyers as they want,"

Logan said, as he filed the flyers with the others in a folder he kept in his backpack. "But we're the only ones who can save their dogs, because only we know what really happened."

"How do you know that?" Aggy asked. "Maybe the police are investigating, too."

"The police don't investigate lost dogs," Logan said.

"No, it's the duty of little kids like us," Kian said.

"What if we told them what we know?" Thatcher said. "Wouldn't they investigate if they knew it was aliens stealing the dogs?"

"They wouldn't believe us, even though we have airtight evidence. We're just kids."

"Maybe it really is someone playing pranks," Aggy said. "You know, unbuckling dogs from their collars, then rebuckling them . . ."

"Most dogs wouldn't run away," Logan said. "Like Festus. Would he have run away if some kid unhooked him?"

Aggy didn't answer. She pulled off her backpack and took out *Ginger Pye*.

"It would be a really mean prank to let

people's dogs go," Thatcher said. "You think maybe they opened Kian's fence, too, so Chloe could get out?"

"But she came back," Aggy said, opening her book at the bookmark.

"And blew my chance at getting a real dog . . ." Kian said, glumly.

"You could adopt Smoky," Thatcher said.

"Smoky's mine," Aggy said.

"Nobody better try to let Bear go," Thatcher said. "He'd tear an alien to pieces. Bear's a maniac."

"Like his owner," Kian said, and gave Thatcher a loud, open-palmed slap to the back.

"Why you!" Thatcher said, swinging back, but missing.

Kian got in another quick slap, then danced out of reach.

"Will you guys knock it off?" Logan said. "We are trying to capture a squad of dognapping aliens here. And some of them live right in that house."

They had arrived at the Sarrises'.

Thatcher abandoned the slap fight. "Darius

and his dad aren't aliens, Logan," he said.

"Are you questioning my skill in identifying alien life-forms?" Logan asked.

Thatcher shrugged. "I guess so. I mean, yeah. I think you're wrong. I don't think Darius is an alien."

Aggy clapped her book shut. "Can you guys stop acting like idiots and let's just get the dogs back?"

21. Mind Control

They hid behind some nearby bushes and watched and waited for the hairy guy to appear. Half an hour went by. Then forty-five minutes.

Logan didn't mind. He was used to waiting and watching. Aggy had her book but was nearing its end.

Kian and Thatcher, however, were done waiting and watching after ten minutes. By the hour mark, they were bored out of their minds.

"Soccer's way better than this," Thatcher groaned.

"Piano is better than this," Kian said, and smacked the back of Thatcher's head.

Thatcher smacked him back.

"Get out of here, you apes," Logan whispered. "You'll blow our cover."

Kian puffed hard into Thatcher's face, making Thatcher's long hair lift.

"There," he said. "I blew your cover." He laughed, then took off running.

Thatcher ran after him.

"Good," Logan said. "I hope they don't come back."

"I have a question, Logan," Aggy asked. "Can the alien make people vanish, too?"

"Absolutely," Logan said.

"So if Mr. Sarris is really the alien, do you think it's a good idea to make him mad? He doesn't like you, Logan."

"I know how to defend myself against an alien," Logan said, and tapped his forehead with his finger. "I have mind control. They can't do anything to you if you have control over your mind. Which I do. Do you, Aggy? You better start practicing. Tell yourself, 'I will not be zapped by an alien. I will not be zapped by an alien. I will not be zapped by an alien.' . . ."

"You *must* be kidding," Aggy said.

"I recommend you work on concentrating your thoughts. Unless, that is, you want to see the inside of an alien spacecraft."

"Concentrate your thoughts on that," Aggy said, pointing at a small gray car coming down the street.

It pulled into the Sarrises' driveway and stopped. Mr. Sarris got out the driver's side, his son, the other.

"Be back by five," Mr. Sarris said, and walked toward the house.

"That the alien's son, Darius," Logan whispered to Aggy.

"Mm-hm," she said. "I've seen him before, playing with a drumming group in the park."

Logan gasped when Darius pulled open the garage door.

"What is it?" Aggy asked. "What do you see?"

"Nothing," Logan said. "I was just expecting to see something."

"Hoping to, you mean."

Darius wheeled out a black BMX with red tires. He put on a black bike helmet with red skulls printed on the sides, straddled his bike, and coasted down the driveway. In the street, facing the bush where Logan and Aggy were hiding, he skidded to a stop.

"What are you doing in there?" he asked.

Logan stepped out from behind the bush.

"I think you know," Logan said to the boy.

"Checking out the aliens?"

"Correct," Logan said.

Aggy stepped out. "Sorry about him, Darius. I'm Aggy."

"Your dad stole her dog," Logan said with a sneer.

"I don't think my dad is your dog thief," Darius said.

"Oh? Why is that?"

"Because our dog disappeared, too."

"Really?" Logan said, skeptically. "Then I guess your dad would have a motive to steal dogs, wouldn't he?"

"Huh?" Darius and Aggy said at the same time.

"To replace the one he lost," Logan said.

"Is he always like this?" Darius asked Aggy.

"Oh, no, not you again!" came a voice from the house. Darius's father stepped out onto the front porch. "I don't want you around here! You called me alien! And dog thief!"

"It's okay, Dad," Darius said. "We're leaving."

"You're going to spend time with this boy? This crazy boy who insults your father?"

"No. I'm going to escort him off the property. Then I'm going to the library to do some research."

"I need to go there, too," Aggy said. "I'm writing an essay on Neptune."

"Mine's on volcanoes," Darius said.

"Let's go then," Aggy said.

"You are falling for the oldest trick in the book, Aggy," Logan said.

"What trick?"

"He wants you to think he's just another kid. But he isn't."

"Okay," Darius said. "Time to go."

Kian burst through a hedge then, followed by Thatcher.

"Hey! Where you guys going? Are you leaving? What's up?" Thatcher asked, out of breath, his hair littered with dried grass and leaves. "Hey, Darius! How's it going?"

"Hey, Thatcher," Darius answered.

"We're going to the library," Aggy said. She hooked Logan's arm. "All three of us."

"What?" Logan said.

"Cool," Thatcher said with a hair toss. Some leaves fluttered free. "You coming with us, Darius?"

"Who's this guy, Thatch?" Kian asked out of the corner of his mouth, eyeing Darius warily.

"I'm the alien's son," Darius said with a smile.

"No, you're not, dude," Thatcher laughed. "Don't believe him, Kian. Darius is cool." He gave the new boy a heavy slap on the shoulder.

"Oh, he's cool," Kian said, his jaw tight. "Cool."

22. The First Puppy

"Aren't you coming in?" Aggy asked Logan in front of the library. Thatcher, Kian, and Darius walked on.

"No. If I can't stake out the Sarrises' house, I'll stake out Sandwiches. At least two dogs have been taken from there. I'm betting Mr. Sarris shows up again. This time I'll stop him."

"I really think he's a regular guy, Logan. Just because he's hairy and wasn't born in America doesn't make him—"

"An alien?" Logan asked with a smirk.

"Not the kind you mean," Aggy said, and walked away.

Logan moved over to his tree to set up.

It was that time again, between school and dinner, when a lot of people converged on Sandwiches, including people with dogs. Logan watched as they patted their dogs good-bye, told them to be good, to be quiet, and to stay, or tied them to the bike rack or the BUS STOP sign or a bench. Some of the dogs waited patiently, panting, their long tongues curling. A few whimpered. One, a clumsy, tawny puppy with big paws, whined loudly and pitiably. People came over and petted it, some spoke baby talk to it. The pup calmed down until they left, then resumed whining. Logan noted all of this on his clipboard.

In time, his friends and Darius reemerged from the library. Aggy was carrying *Pinky Pye*, the sequel to *Ginger Pye*.

"Did you see anything suspicious?" Kian asked Logan.

Logan shook his head, then, speaking to Darius, added, "I haven't seen your dad."

"Stop that, Logan," Aggy said. "It's not funny, and it's not nice."

"I'm not trying to be funny or nice," Logan said.

"Don't worry about it," Darius said. "He probably just feels bad about not having a dad of his own."

Logan whirled around. "What did you say?" he said, leaning in close to Darius.

"I say we should stop talking about each other's dads."

Logan glowered at Thatcher, then Kian, wondering which had revealed personal information about him to Darius.

"You're not watching the store," Aggy said.

Logan huffed, then returned to his stakeout.

"Hey," he said, after lifting his binoculars to his eyes. "Where's the puppy?"

"What puppy?" Thatcher asked. "Where was it? Was it stolen?"

"There was a puppy tied up outside the door just a second ago," Logan said. "Now it's gone."

"Its owner came out and got him?" Darius suggested.

"Yeah, probably," Aggy said, but her voice was tainted with doubt.

"It wasn't its owner that got him," Logan said. "Come on, Crew!" And he ran toward the store, his backpack bouncing behind him as he went.

"Is he serious?" Darius asked Aggy. "He really

thinks a dog was stolen in the split second he looked away?"

"That's how it happened with Festus." Her eyes widened.

"Come on!" she said, and ran after Logan. The three boys fell in behind her.

23. The Chairnapper

When Logan reached the store's entrance, he found a woman in brightly colored Lycra bike clothes glancing about, a confused look on her face.

"Was it your pup, ma'am?" Logan asked.

"Pardon me?" she said.

"Your pup, ma'am. Was it yours?"

"She must have gotten loose. . . ."

"Is this her collar, ma'am?" Logan asked, lifting a yellow leather collar attached to a nylon lead, the other end of which was tied to the bike rack.

The woman looked at it. "Yes, that's Nilla's."

Logan dropped the collar and walked past her into the store, confident he'd find Mr. Sarris there. He peered down the store's four aisles, checking out the deli and the produce section. No hairy guy.

When he was running back out of the front door, he slammed into Darius.

"Whoa, there," Darius said.

"You!" Logan said. "Where's your dad?"

"I thought we talked about this."

"He has to be around . . . ," Logan said, and ran off down the sidewalk.

The woman began calling, "Nilla! Nilla! Where are you, Nilla!"

Aggy recognized the woman's growing panic and tried to comfort her. "It's okay. We'll find her. We'll find her."

"Yeah, don't worry," Thatcher added. "We're the Canine Rescue Unit. The Crew. We're on it."

"Right," Kian said.

"The what?" Darius asked.

A couple of blocks away, Logan spotted the old man in the electric wheelchair rolling along the sidewalk. Logan was supposed to be looking for the puppy thief, but he couldn't pass up the opportunity to compare the wheelchair to the one pictured in the flyer. He had it with him this time, in his backpack.

"Excuse me, sir!" he called, running toward the man. "Excuse me!"

Instead of stopping, the wheelchair accelerated.

Logan did, too.

"Wait, sir!" he yelled. "I only want to ask you a question!"

At the corner, the wheelchair turned sharply to the right, so sharply the chair's left wheels momentarily lifted off the ground.

"Whoa! Careful!" Logan yelled.

Though he was pretty sure he was now in pursuit of a thief of a different kind—not a dognapper, but a chairnapper—Logan didn't want to see an old man thrown from his speeding, motorized mobility aid.

He cut the chairnapper off by crossing diagonally through the parking lot of an alternative medical center, then planted himself in the middle of the sidewalk, blocking the wheelchair's path. The old man let go of the joystick, and the wheelchair slowed to a stop.

The man wore the same dark blue stocking cap as before. This time he had no paper to duck behind, and his huge, dark sunglasses had slid down to the tip of his long, sloped nose. His eyes were extremely far apart, and their large, dusky irises practically crowded out all the white. His mouth was broad, his lips sucked in, his chin knobby and bare, save for the fine gray whiskers that covered most of his face. He was hunched in his chair, his narrow shoulders wrapped in a plaid shawl, wheezing softly but rapidly. This wheezing led Logan to look again at the man's nose, which was when he noticed that the man had no nostrils.

"You again," the man said, though his mouth remained shut. A faint amber glow pulsed beneath his chin.

"Hello, sir," Logan said. "I wanted to ask you—"

The man's mouth suddenly gaped wide, revealing long rows of small, rounded teeth and a big, pink, triangular tongue that tightened and vibrated.

Logan blacked out.

24. Big Blue Balloon

Hovering dogs. That's what Logan saw when he awoke. Hovering dogs, tumbling and twisting in the air, some paddling their legs as if in slow motion, others just drifting. They were not easy to count, but Logan put their number at between ten and thirteen.

Logan was also hovering. Like the dogs, he floated in midair, weightless and naked.

"This must be a dream," he said, his words sounding gurgly, as if they came from his mouth inside bubbles.

He had the sense he was floating in a room of some kind, but that the blue-hued walls, floor, and ceiling were translucent and elastic. He was trapped inside a big blue balloon filled with blue Jell-O.

Whatever it was that kept Logan and the dogs aloft—was it a liquid? a gas? something in between?—it was breathable, like air, and gave them the ability to defy gravity. Which was not unpleasant. In fact, it was fun.

Some of the dogs were making their way toward Logan, dog paddling through the air, and so he attempted to meet them halfway, via the breaststroke. It was slow going through the gummy air. Kicking his feet helped.

The first dog he met was Pickles, the dog that had vanished out of her collar as Logan was boarding the school bus. He offered her his open hand. She sniffed his fingers, then licked them.

"Hi, Pickles," he gurgled.

Other dogs arrived, some that Logan recognized from the flyers, including a little Pomeranian mix: Ollie. And there was Nilla, the puppy that had disappeared from Sandwiches. It had been while looking for Nilla's thief that Logan had come across the old man in the wheelchair, and chased him down, and discovered what a very odd-looking man he was; how, in fact, he had . . .

"No nostrils," Logan said aloud.

He remembered the old man opening his huge mouth.

"Maybe the old guy conked me on the head. Maybe he knocked me unconscious. Maybe he's the dognapper? He was at Sandwiches when Festus disappeared. He was the only one around, in fact. Did he beam me here? Did he beam the dogs? Is this his spaceship?"

The dogs began to bark and wag their tails sluggishly through the water. Logan sensed there was someone behind him and spun around to find a creature swiftly and gracefully approaching him. It was bigger than a dog, as big as a man. When it was upon him, Logan saw it had a gray face, with wide-set eyes, a sloped nose, and a broad grin. It was the face of the old man in the wheelchair. The body attached to it was not wearing a sweatsuit or a shawl. It was not wearing anything. It had flippers. And a tail.

The old man was a dolphin.

25. Flipper Fingers

The dolphin circled twice, then rose into a vertical position, face-to-face with Logan. Its expression did not seem angry. It seemed curious.

Pickles swam to the creature and licked its face. The creature made a shrill, chipper, gurgling sound.

Upon closer inspection, Logan found reasons to question his conclusion that the creature was a dolphin—or, at least, a dolphin from Earth. The creature had flippers, for example, but on the tip of each it had fingers and a thumb. Its body was long and sleek, but its lower half was separated into two legs with no knees and flukes at the end. The dorsal fin was short and blunt, as was its beak—blunt enough to allow the creature to pass as human, Logan thought.

"You aren't a dolphin, are you?" Logan asked.

A small dot of golden light glowed from the alien's throat, as if through its skin.

"No," the creature replied. Its beak didn't open and close when it spoke, the sound coming more from its throat than its mouth. The voice was less shrill and chipper than before, less dolphiny, more human sounding. All of this made Logan suspicious.

"Is that a translation device in your throat?" he asked, pointing at the golden spot.

The creature nodded deeply, almost bowing, which afforded Logan a view of the blowhole on top of its head.

"You're not from Earth, are you?" Logan asked.

Again the golden spot glowed, and the creature replied, "I am not."

"What planet are you from?"

"I can tell you what it is called," the alien said, "but I don't think you'll be able to hear it. The name is spoken at a frequency higher than humans can hear."

"I'd like to hear it anyway."

The alien opened its mouth. Its pink, triangular tongue tightened and vibrated, as it had before Logan blacked out.

The dogs howled.

"You were right," he said. "I couldn't hear it."

"The dogs could," the alien said.

"Are you male or female?" Logan asked. "Or do you have something else on your planet?"

"Female."

"Do you have a name?"

"Not one you can hear."

"I'll just say 'ma'am,' then."

"What is 'ma'am'?"

"It's the polite word for a woman."

"I see."

"Why did you come to Earth, ma'am?" Logan asked.

"We came because you have water, and an atmosphere with oxygen. We were on a treasure-seeking mission. My employer wanted to stop to see if there was anything of interest on your planet, anything we might bring home and sell."

"And your employer liked our dogs?"

"Yes. We don't have dogs on our planet."

"So your boss started beaming them here?"

"What is 'beaming'?"

"Zapping them. Disintegrating them and then reintegrating them."

The light in her throat glowed longer for this one, as if extra translation was required.

"That is not precisely how it's done," she said, "but yes, my employer has been sending the dogs here."

"How is it done . . . precisely?" Logan asked.

"It involves sound. High-frequency sounds. We produce, and can hear, much higher sounds than humans. Like your dolphins. And your dogs. That is one of the things my employer likes about your dogs. They can hear us."

"Why don't you steal dolphins?"

"My employer says the dolphins are too similar to us. Yet primitive."

"Interesting," Logan said, and reached back for his clipboard to make some notes, when he remembered he didn't have his backpack. It was back on Earth. With his clothes.

"Where is your employer, ma'am?"

"In your town. He poses as an old man."

"Aha!" Logan said. "So you're not him. You're a second alien!"

He had assumed wrong: this was not the alien in the wheelchair. He had also assumed right, though: there was more than one.

"You look a lot like your boss, ma'am," he said.

"Maybe to human eyes," the alien said.

"Do you go to Earth, too, and steal dogs?"

The alien shook her head. "No, I wouldn't do that. I stay here and take care of them."

She reached out and scratched the top of Pickles's head. Pickles panted.

"They like you, don't they, ma'am?"

"I like them."

Logan thought he detected a smile on her face. Unfortunately, the alien's mouth, like the mouth of the creature she resembled, always seemed to be grinning.

"Does your boss plan to take over Earth, ma'am?" Logan asked.

"No. He just wants to take the dogs."

"*All* of them?"

"No. Only as many as we can carry."

"What about me?" Logan asked. "Are you going to take me?"

The alien didn't answer.

"You're going to send me home, aren't you?" Logan asked, his voice starting to shake.

It hit him that it was possible he would not see his home—his mom, his friends, his dog, his *planet*—ever again, that he had really been abducted by aliens and was being held prisoner in outer space. *Outer space.* While this was tremendously exciting to Logan, it was also absolutely terrifying.

The alien flapped her flippers, causing her to drift away from him.

"What *are* you going to do with me, ma'am?" His fear was rapidly transforming into anger.

The alien retreated farther.

"I want to go *home*!" Logan screamed. *"Now!"*

With a single, mighty beat of her legs, the alien was gone.

26. Return of the Fourth Dog

Logan paddled in the direction the alien had fled. It was slow going, but eventually he came to one of the blue, translucent, elastic walls. It was springy to the touch. He pressed his face to it, straining to see what was on the other side, but saw only a slowly churning indigo murk, like blue ink, or deep space.

He groped about but could find no opening in the wall. Maybe the alien had opened it with high-frequency sound. Or maybe she had simply ultrasonically transported herself to another part of the ship.

Logan punched the wall in frustration, and his fist bounced back and slugged him in the stomach. He hollered, not in pain but in fury.

"Let me out of here! I'm *seeeri*ous! You can't keep me! This is kidnapping! It's illegal! When the FBI finds out, you'll go to jail! Probably for *life*!"

The dogs responded with a mournful chorus of howling and whining, which turned his anger at his predicament into indignation.

"How dare they steal our dogs," he said, less wildly, his jaw set, his eyes narrowed. "How *dare* they!"

As he swam back to the dogs, he realized it was his duty to thwart the aliens' plot. He must return the dogs safely to their grieving owners, and return himself to his mother, who was surely overcome with worry. She probably had sent out mass e-mails, and put up flyers of her own, ones that read LOST BOY instead of LOST DOG. She probably cried as she stapled them to telephone poles.

This image made Logan's eyes tear up.

Some of the dogs rushed to his side, whimpering and pawing at him. The puppy, Nilla, licked his face.

"You don't like it when I yell," he said, "but you come when I cry."

Others swam to him and licked his face, lapped up his tears, and raised his spirits. He giggled, which caused more to swarm him.

"And you really like it when I'm happy!" he said, laughing.

He had to get them home, back to Earth, but how? The only way he could think of was ultra-sonic transport, to return them the way they—and he—had come. But he had no idea how this beaming up and down, to and fro, was done, or how he could possibly perform such an other-worldly act. After all, he couldn't make high-frequency sounds.

"*You* can, though," he said to the dogs. "Maybe you can howl us back to Earth!"

He said this with such elation that the dogs went into fits of yipping and began wagging their hindquarters. They scuttled in close to Logan, and piled on him the best they could, considering they were afloat. It was during this aerial puppy rumpus that Logan saw Aggy's dog.

"Come here, Festus!" Logan called.

The old beagle tried, but his feebleness pre-vented him from making any real progress. So

Logan broke free of the swarm and dogpaddled to him. He hugged Festus around the neck, and the dog's tongue flopped out of his mouth.

"I'm going to get you out of here, boy," Logan said. "I promise."

He would need help from someone who knew how the beaming was done, someone who could perform it.

Logan recalled how the alien had said she liked the dogs. She also said she "wouldn't do that" when Logan asked her if she'd stolen dogs, too. He felt she did not condone the dognappings, nor his kidnapping, that she didn't like what her boss was up to. She might be the ally he needed.

But he had screamed at her, frightened her away.

"Control your temper, Logan," his mom often counseled him. Coached him. "Count to a hundred by twos. Alphabetize the aliens in *Star Wars*. That should take a while."

Sometimes these strategies worked, and he did calm himself down, but, secretly, he didn't like controlling his temper. He liked to let it rage, like a wildfire. He liked to bellow and roar, like a

Wookiee. It made him feel strong and fierce. He disliked his mom's attempts to calm him, to tame him, to make him be nice.

Still, he figured he'd better try to control his temper around the alien, to be calm and polite. Adults liked politeness. Especially women. They liked "thank you," "no, thank you," and "please."

He felt his politeness had worked with the alien, too (maybe politeness was universal?), but then his outburst had undone all his work. He was going to have to keep a lid on his temper if he hoped to liberate himself and the dogs.

He was determined to succeed.

27. Hover Planet

The female alien soon returned, this time gripping a small pouch in her flipper hand. The pouch was made of a material much like the walls and ceiling: translucent, blue, gelatinous. It looked to Logan like a jellyfish minus the tentacles; it inflated and deflated like one, too.

The alien swam around the dogs, using the pouch to collect their business (as Logan's mom referred to it), both solid and liquid, which hung in the air in clumps or as glistening amber threads. She avoided swimming near Logan, or even glancing at him.

"Excuse me, ma'am," he called to her.

Now she glanced, but only briefly, as she continued her work.

"I'm very sorry I shouted at you, ma'am,"

Logan said. "It was very impolite of me. I hope you'll forgive me. It's just that I'm . . ." He didn't relish completing the sentence, here or anywhere, whether he meant it or not, but he knew it would help his cause, so he said, "I'm scared."

The alien paused in her work and turned toward him. Her long mouth curved downward for a change, in sympathy, exactly what Logan had hoped for.

"You see, I've never been kidnapped before," he said, drooping his head forlornly. This act wasn't difficult. It was how he truly felt. The trick actually was not to feel it too keenly, to avoid getting so sad and scared that he became angry and frustrated. "I miss my mom, and she's probably worried sick."

The alien flicked her flukes and, in an instant, was beside him.

"I understand," she said, tentatively reaching out her silvery hands.

He wanted to be held, to be comforted, but not necessarily by an alien life-form. Nor by his jailer. Unsure of how she would react, he recoiled.

She withdrew her hands but did not leave.

"I miss my friends, too, and my dog, Bubba," Logan said, steeling himself against his own words, speaking them but not letting their full meaning sink in, for he really did ache to see his friends, his dog, his mom, his brother. . . .

"I would very much like to go home, please, ma'am," he said.

The alien's frown deepened and her eyes moistened.

The buoyant dog herd moved in, ready to help.

"Bubba's my best friend," Logan said. "I don't know what I'll do without her. Or what she'll do without me. She needs me to feed her, and clean up after her, and love her, like you do for these dogs, the ones you're holding captive."

He wasn't sure about that last part. He wanted her to empathize with him, and also to feel bad about her role in his predicament, but he didn't want her to feel so guilty she would swim away again.

The alien's throat light glowed at his words, translating them, but she did not respond. She sagged into a posture Logan recognized in humans. If it was the same for the alien's kind, she was feeling ashamed.

Logan decided he had gotten his message across, and it was time to change the subject.

"Why does your boss ride in a wheelchair?"

Again the alien's light lit, but she didn't reply.

"Ma'am?" Logan asked, as if concerned.

She shook off her distressing thoughts. "It's difficult for him to walk on your planet. Your air is thin, and your gravity, strong."

"Did he steal the wheelchair, too?"

The female alien nodded.

"The woman he stole it from posted a flyer," Logan said, building his case that her boss was a lowlife thief whom she should defy. Again this was not difficult to do, as it was what Logan really believed. "She offered a reward for it. She was old and couldn't get around without it, but couldn't afford a new one. They cost a lot of Earth money."

The alien gave a little pout, which Logan viewed as a good sign. She cared about others, even people she had never met. That made her more likely to help him and the dogs.

"Where does he keep the wheelchair and clothes when he's here?" Logan asked, adding, "I assume he stole the clothes as well. . . ."

He was only assuming the boss alien returned to the ship periodically. Wouldn't he want to check on things? Wasn't that what bosses do? And wouldn't he want to shed his clothes and his wheelchair, escape Earth's atmosphere and gravity, and relax, as parents do when returning home from work?

"He hides them in a park," the alien said. "Inside a cave, by the beach."

Logan figured it was Ketchoklam Park. It was the only park in town with a beach.

"I see," he said. "Does he come up from Earth every day?"

"We are on Earth," the alien said.

"We *are*? Where?"

"Submerged in the bay beside your town."

"Is that why we float?" Logan asked. "I thought we were weightless because we were in space."

"We float because the ship is filled with air from our planet," the alien explained. "Our air is heavier, which is why we don't walk on the ground. We hover."

"Interesting," Logan said. "Yet me and the dogs can breathe it. . . ."

"Yes. We didn't know if that would be so, but when we brought the first dog here . . ."

Her face darkened again, and Logan believed he knew why.

"That dog was lucky it could breathe your air," Logan said.

"Yes," the alien said distractedly. "Lucky."

"Why don't the authorities know you're here?" Logan asked. He couldn't fathom how the aliens could have landed a spaceship in Nelsonport without being picked up by radar, or lay submerged in the bay without being detected by sonar.

"We are able to neutralize your planet's detection systems," the alien said. "We are more sophisticated when it comes to waves."

"Waves?"

"Sound waves. Radio waves. We're very sensitive to them. And we interact with them differently than you."

"Impressive," Logan said.

The alien showed no pride. Her thoughts were plainly elsewhere, which pleased Logan. Her conscience was eating at her. Logan took advantage of this.

"I'm pretty hungry, ma'am," he said, which was, also, conveniently true. "This is the time I would usually sit down to dinner with my mom and my little brother. He's only one and seven-twelfths years old." Logan nearly added, "I sure miss the little guy," but sensed that would be going too far.

"I have a younger brother, too," the alien said. "Back home. I miss him."

"I'm sure you do," Logan said.

It was good she had a family of her own. She could relate to his predicament. Plus, she would want to be heading home soon.

Logan laid his hand on the alien in the area where a human shoulder would be, ignoring the uneasiness he felt about coming into physical contact with a creature from another galaxy. There was no telling what diseases, for example, he might open himself up to. She tensed a bit but did not shrink away. She let him comfort her.

Logan smiled, feeling confident he was half-way home. But abruptly the alien pulled away. She opened her mouth wide, and her tongue tightened.

"Is something wrong, ma'am?" he asked. "What's happening?"

She snapped her mouth shut. Her eyes showed dread. Her throat light glowed, and her humanoid voice intoned, "He's coming."

28. Aliens Don't Smell

The boss alien materialized right in front of them. It happened quick as a blink. No one there; alien there. Like a camcorder trick: shoot the background; pause; have a friend move into the shot; unpause; stop; watch it back; friend materializes out of thin air.

Without his wheelchair and clothes, the boss alien did not seem old at all. He seemed young, strong, vital—and angry.

He chattered at his underling in a sharp, shrill voice that reminded Logan more of a chimpanzee than a dophin.

"I was busy," the female alien said, her mouth, as usual not opening and shutting, her throat light glowing, "with the boy. Why did you send a boy here?"

Her boss shrieked louder and higher until his voice rose to such a pitch that Logan could no longer hear it. The alien's beak, however, continued to clap.

"What are we going to do with him?" the female alien asked in reply.

Her boss got quite agitated at this, flapping his fins vigorously and getting right up in her face.

"Oh . . . I forgot . . . sorry . . . ," she said, then opened her mouth and tightened her tongue. The golden light went out. The remainder of their heated argument was conducted out of the range of Logan's hearing.

The male alien continued clapping his beak in the female alien's direction, until, as she did with Logan, she could take no more and swam off. She didn't exit the chamber, though; she went back to scooping poop—her version of counting to a hundred by twos, Logan thought.

"Excuse me, sir," Logan said to her boss.

The alien whirled on him, his broad mouth twisted in a grimace, his amber throat light glowing.

"What do you want?" he demanded. His English-speaking voice was the same as his assistant's: the voice of the translating device, a monotone, machinelike voice.

"I'm sorry to bother you, sir," Logan continued, trying to pretend he wasn't terrified, "but I have a couple of questions."

"Only a couple?" the alien asked.

"Are you guys fighting about me?" Logan asked.

The alien huffed through his blowhole the way a human would through its nostrils. It created turbulence in the blue, alien air over his head.

"I'm sorry, sir," Logan said. "I don't mean to cause trouble."

"You don't mean to cause trouble? Weren't you, in fact, determined to cause trouble? Isn't that what you were doing with your binoculars and camera and clipboard? Weren't you trying to root out the dog thief, which, for some reason, you were convinced was from another planet?"

Hearing that the alien knew what he had been doing in such detail took Logan aback, but he tried not to show it.

"Yes, I was," he said. "And I did root you out, sir. And you are from another planet, sir."

"But you did not stop me, or rescue the dogs, did you? And you didn't know that I was the thief. You were following someone else, the 'hairy guy,' who was completely innocent."

Logan didn't like admitting he was wrong, but he couldn't deny it. "Yes, sir," he said. "I was mistaken."

"You also didn't know the alien you were hunting could hear your private conversations from a considerable distance."

"Really?" Logan said. "How far?"

"Far," the alien said with self-satisfaction. "A mile or more."

"Wow," Logan added, noting that the alien enjoyed flattery.

"I doubted you were a threat," the alien went on. "One thing I've learned about humans is that the adults rarely believe, or even listen to, the stories children tell. They assume that when a story is implausible, the child's imagination has gone wild, or that the child's inexperience has affected its reason. I've overheard many conversations in which an adult humors a child, or pretends to listen, or doesn't listen at all."

"My mom believed me about you."

"I disagree. She didn't *dis*believe you, but she didn't believe you. Your bus driver didn't believe you, either, nor did your friends—this 'Intergalactic Canine Rescue Unit' of yours."

"I don't know about that, sir," Logan said, a bit dismayed at hearing this. "I think Aggy was beginning to believe me. And Thatcher definitely did. . . ."

"That's not important," the alien said, his temper rising again. "What's important is that you chased me down and confronted me. That was too much. I couldn't afford to let you get close enough to get a good look at me. So I removed you."

"But you left clues, sir," Logan said. "My backpack . . . my clothes . . ."

"I am not stupid, boy. I collected your things and hid them where no one will find them."

"But you left the collars and leashes. Why?"

"I left them only when taking the time to untie a leash might result in my being caught," the alien said with irritation. "Not that I worried much. I never actually had a stolen dog in my possession. I was just an old man in a wheelchair. How could I steal a dog? The costume proved to be the perfect disguise. No one ever paid attention to me. In fact, people tended to avoid looking at me."

"It was a brilliant disguise," Logan said, recalling how he had dismissed the old man without a second thought. "I commend you, sir."

The alien dipped his head, which Logan took to be a bow. Yes, he thought, the guy really likes praise.

"Can I ask another question, sir?" Logan asked. "Why didn't you take my dog? Was it because she farts?"

"That would make no difference to us," the alien said. "We don't have olfactory organs. We can't smell."

"Oh," Logan said. He remembered learning once that owls couldn't smell, which was why they could hunt skunks. He wondered if dolphins had olfactory organs.

"So then why didn't you take Bubba?" he asked.

"I figured that if I did, you would redouble your efforts to thwart my plans."

"But you took Kian's dog, Chloe. And Aggy's dog, Festus."

The alien smirked. "I didn't take Chloe. What an annoying little beast. She must have gotten out on her own. And I took Festus because I overheard your argument with the so-called 'hairy man.' I was attempting to strengthen your belief that he was an alien."

Logan nodded. "So now you have all these dogs, and one boy. What do you do now?"

"I still have room for more dogs," the alien said.

"But dare you steal more from Nelsonport, sir?" Logan said, starting to enjoy this confrontation with an invader from outer space, the dolphinlike dog thief from another planet. "Maybe my friends didn't believe me before, but I'm sure they do now. They will be looking for you."

Malice smoldered in the alien's eyes. "If they find me, or get close to finding me," he said, "they will end up here with you."

This punctured Logan's swelling confidence. "And what would you do with all of us then?" he asked in a meeker voice. "Would you take us to your planet?"

The alien's menacing grin curled at the ends.

Logan imagined his friends appearing in the hold, one by one, and how it would be his fault, how it would be because they listened to him and trusted him that they would never see their families or homes again. He thought in particular of Aggy, and how crushed she was by the loss of Festus, but how much more crushed she would be when she realized the aliens had abducted her, too, and that she would never return to Earth, and her family, again.

And it was then, as Logan was thinking of Aggy and Festus, that a solution popped into his head.

29. Tap Noses on It

"I would like to make a proposal, sir," Logan said to the alien. "But before I do, can you ask your employee to come back in here?"

He wasn't sure whether the boss alien had feelings to appeal to, whether he cared at all where he got his dogs or who got hurt in the process. He was resentful of Logan, had kidnapped him, and appeared poised to take Logan from his home forever, or worse. Logan thought the female would see the genius behind his proposal, because she not only cared about the dogs and about Logan, but also because she felt bad about stealing them and wanted to do the right thing.

"Why?" the male alien asked.

"It involves her," Logan said, which didn't

seem true when he said it, but the more he thought about it, the more true it became.

"How does it involve her?" the alien asked.

"Call her in and you'll see," Logan said.

The alien again huffed through his blowhole, then called for his assistant, in the usual ultrasonic way.

She swam in, her head low, her eyes averted. Logan could see she was afraid of her boss.

"What if I told you there were places with enough dogs to fill this room," Logan said, "and you wouldn't have to steal them?"

"Are there such places?" the female alien asked, her expression brightening a little.

"There are," Logan said, folding his arms on his chest proudly. "We call them animal shelters. They're places that take in homeless or abused animals and try to find homes for them."

"People abuse their dogs?"

"I'm afraid so. But some just change their minds about having a dog and abandon them. Sometimes they're found and taken to a shelter. Other times people bring them to a shelter themselves."

"Is there one of these animal shelters in your town?" the male alien asked.

"There is," Logan said. "It's out near the land-fill. Too far for you to hear, I guess."

"Can you take me there?"

"I could, but only if you promise me something."

"You want me to return the dogs."

"And me. Send us back, and I'll show you where the shelter is. I'm sure they'll have more dogs than you captured. And they'll have cats, too."

"What's a cat?" asked the female alien.

"I don't care for cats," her boss said.

"Me, neither," Logan said.

"How would we get there?"

"Can't you just beam yourself there? You know, ultrasonically?"

"One of us would have to be there in order to do that. Sound transport requires a sender and a receiver."

"How do you get to town then, if your assistant stays here?" Logan asked.

"We have portable sound transmitters that

can send or receive signals," the female alien said.

"I've hidden some around town in secluded places," her boss said. "To help me get around."

"Do you have any near my house?" Logan asked.

"How do you know I know where you live?"

"You do. You can hear things from far away. You know where I live. And I bet there's a transmitter hidden near it."

An arch grin came over the alien's face. "You are a bright boy."

"Thank you, sir."

"And so polite," the female alien said. "I wish my son was as polite."

"I didn't know you had a son, ma'am. You must miss him terribly."

"I do," she said, and looked away.

"Well, let's go get those dogs and fill up this thing and send you back to him," Logan said.

"Wait," the male alien said. "You didn't say how we would get to the shelter."

"I'll get you there, don't worry. I'm bright, remember? But first you must promise to set me and the dogs free."

"How do I know I can trust you? How do I know you won't lead me into a trap?"

"Because if you return the dogs, you will no longer be a dognapper. I'll have no reason to turn you in. You can take the shelter's dogs and fly back to your planet and find them homes."

"Please return the dogs, sir," the female alien said. "And Logan, too. It isn't right to take them. They have homes. Families. They are loved, and missed."

"And if no one adopts the dogs in the shelter," Logan interjected, "they will be euthanized."

"Killed?" the female alien asked.

"You'll be doing the shelter and the dogs a favor by giving them good homes. Even if it is on another planet."

Logan asked, "So do we have a deal?"

The alien squinted at him. Logan squinted back. He worried the alien would try to take both the dognapped dogs and the shelter dogs back to his planet. He would have to proceed carefully.

"Understand, human," the alien said, "any time I wish, I can transport you back here."

"I understand," Logan said.

"Then we have a deal," the alien said, and with a brisk flap of his fins, he swam up close to Logan, beak to nose.

Logan pulled back.

"We tap noses on our planet when we make a deal," the alien explained.

"We shake hands," Logan said.

They did both.

30. Bubba

The next moment, Logan found himself sprawled out on the dirt floor of an old, dilapidated shed. Dusky light slanted in through the spaces between the shed's boards. Cold air entered the same way.

Nelsonport had many such sheds. Long ago they had housed horse-drawn carriages. Now they stood on empty lots amid tall weeds and NO TRESPASSING signs, leaning and rotting, their roofs heavy with moss, till the day the brittle, aging nails could no longer bear the strain, and the structures collapsed into piles of splintered wood.

Logan silently commended the alien on his choice of landing stage. The shed was so rickety no one would dare enter it.

"Good hiding place, ma'am," he said, his voice

clear and bubble-free again, but his teeth chattering.

Her boss had agreed to the deal, but had chosen to send his underling on the mission, too. He preferred remaining with his ship and his loot—the stolen dogs—to making the arduous trip to uncharted territory with Logan, who might have tricks up his sleeve.

Logan was relieved to be traveling with the female alien, whom he viewed as an ally, rather than with her surly superior.

"Thank you," his companion's translation device said. It sounded crisper in Earth's thinner air.

Logan gave her credit for courage. She had agreed to come to a foreign planet, where she was quite vulnerable, and, if found out, she could potentially never escape.

"Where's the transmitter?" Logan asked.

The alien peered around the shed.

"There," she said, pointing a flipper.

"That old can?" Logan asked, and picked up a tin can thick with rust.

"No, next to it," the alien said. "The nail."

Logan lifted an equally rusted nail.

"That's it."

"Stay here," Logan said. "I need to get a few things from my house."

The alien's forehead furrowed.

"Trust me," Logan said. "I'll be right back. Stay out of sight."

He stepped outside the shed without waiting for a response and immediately recognized where he was: at the end of the alley that ran behind his house. He shot down the alley in the fading daylight, ninja-style: quiet, hunched over, trying to stay out of sight below the line of the back fences. When he reached his house, he pushed aside a big, black plastic garbage can and scaled the wooden fence to his backyard.

The house was dark, but maybe his mom just hadn't gotten around to turning on any lights. Maybe she was sitting on the couch, crying and praying the phone would ring with news about his whereabouts and so hadn't noticed yet that the sun was setting. It seemed more likely to him, though, that she was out driving around the neighborhood, looking for him, her cell phone in her lap. Either way, she would have left Sloane with his grandma, who lived in town, so he wouldn't see his mom crying and upset.

Logan wanted very much to see his mom, but he was fairly certain she would delay him with tears and hugging, with questions, scoldings, and warnings. He couldn't let anything keep him from completing his task. Even his mother. He was hoping she wasn't home.

He ninjaed across the yard to his window. It was open, as usual. He pulled himself up onto the ledge, rolled over it, then dropped, catlike, onto the carpeted floor of his room. When he rose up, he found Bubba lying on the bed. She lazily lifted her head.

"Unnnh, unnnh, unnnh," she said.

Logan rubbed her shoulder. "Where's Mom?" he whispered.

Bubba stared right into his eyes. If she had looked away, toward the kitchen, say, Logan would have known his mom was home. That's how close he and Bubba were.

"That's a good dog," Logan whispered. "I missed you."

Bubba farted.

31. The Co-operative

Logan pulled on a pair of jeans and a long-sleeve T-shirt. He didn't bother with underwear, as he would just be leaving it behind in a few minutes. He grabbed two more shirts and two more pairs of jeans—for later—then crept down the hall to the laundry room. Through its window he could survey the front yard. The car was not parked in the driveway. His mom had gone somewhere, probably looking for him.

Logan dug through the clothes in the drier and pulled out one of his mom's nightgowns. He also dug out a long skirt and a sweatshirt. He ran into the living room, to the phone, and dialed a number.

"Jenny?" the answerer asked, excitedly. "Did you find him?"

"I'm not my mom," Logan said. "I'm me. Logan. Don't say my name. Are you alone?"

"Where have you— What *happened*?"

"Don't let anyone know who you're talking to."

"I'm in my room. No one can hear me."

"Good. Don't talk—listen. I need your help. You must do *exactly* as I say."

"But—"

"Silence! I'm serious. We don't have much time. I found Festus. . . ."

"You *did*!"

"Yes, and we can save him, but we must act swiftly."

"Where is he?"

"If you promise to shut up, I'll tell you."

"Okay, okay. I promise. Tell me where Festus is."

"On a spaceship hiding in the bay."

He waited to see if she would respond.

She didn't.

He went on.

"Ride your bike over here immediately. I need you to carry a transmitter to the animal shelter." He paused. "You may respond."

"What's a transmitter? Why the animal shelter?"

"You'll find out later. I need you to tell me you can be here on your bike within ten minutes. Otherwise I need to call another Crew member."

"It's almost dinnertime. . . ."

"So you cannot. Okay, I'll call—"

"No, I'll come, I'll come! I'll sneak out."

"Good. Meet us by the shed at the end of the alley behind my house."

"Us?"

"Over and out," Logan said, and hung up the phone.

He hesitated a moment, wondering if there was anything else in the house that could come in handy on his mission. He knew he couldn't carry anything with him when he transported. He grabbed a banana from the fruit bowl, then snagged his rubber boots—also for later—on the way out the back door.

As he slinked down the alley, he saw that lights were coming on in his neighbors' houses. Logan saw the people in their kitchens, gathering for dinner.

"After this is over," he whispered to himself, "me and Mom and Sloane will have dinner, too. Mom didn't make anything, so maybe I can convince her to order a pizza."

That was one good thing about having a single mom. She often got so swamped with work, errands, bills, and chauffeuring, she didn't have time to prepare a meal.

Logan wondered about the alien's family life, back on her planet. He knew she had a son, and that she missed him. Did she have other children? Did she have a husband—a mate? Did they live in a house? Did their houses look like Earth houses? Did they float?

They probably didn't have cars on her planet. Why would they need them? They could float. And transport themselves. And transport objects. They wouldn't need trucks or planes or ships. What an amazing world it must be. He wished he could see it.

They didn't have dogs, though. That would make life difficult. Maybe impossible. Not to mention his mom and brother and friends didn't live there. No, as curious as he was about the aliens' planet, he did not want to be taken to it. He wanted to stay on Earth.

"My co-operative is on the way, ma'am," he said to the alien when he was back in the shed.

"Your co-operative?"

"Yes. We are both operatives of the Intergalactic Canine Rescue Unit. She will take the transmitter to the animal shelter. Then you can transport us there."

The alien smiled. "I see. You're very clever."

"Thank you, ma'am. We should wait here in the shed. If I'm seen by anyone I know, they might take me to my mom."

"You don't want to go to your mom?"

"I do, but not yet. Not till the mission is complete. She might not believe me."

"So my boss is right about the adults? They don't trust children? They don't listen to them?"

"You weren't there when he said that. Were you eavesdropping?"

The golden light shone on her throat, but she didn't speak.

"What's wrong?" Logan asked.

"The translator doesn't know that word."

"Eavesdropping? It means listening to other people's conversations when they don't know you're doing it."

"I see. We don't have a word for that. We can't help overhearing. He's listening to us now, I'm sure."

"Well, he's wrong," Logan said. "My mom listens. And she trusts me. Human adults are just very busy taking care of adult things, so they don't always notice what's going on around them, and then when we tell them what's going on, they have trouble believing it because they didn't notice it themselves. They think they're smarter than us, but they're wrong. Actually, thinking you're smarter than someone else is a sign of lesser intelligence. If they were really smarter than us, they would know that."

"You're more than clever," the alien said. "You're wise."

"Thank you, ma'am."

32. Beautiful Alien World

"Who's this?" Aggy asked Logan behind her hand.

The alien was standing in the shed, bracing herself against a beam in the darkened corner and wearing one of Jenny's floor-length nightgowns.

"This is one of the aliens," Logan said, as if he were introducing Aggy to an aunt. "I can't say her name because it's ultrasonic. She's helping me."

"Hello," the alien said. "Pleased to meet you."

Aggy stared. Her expressive eyebrows were unusually slack, and her mouth fell open.

"It's okay, Aggy," Logan said. "She's a good alien. She's helping us."

Aggy shook her head in tiny, rapid movements, as if trying to wake herself from the shock of what she was seeing.

"Aggy!" Logan snapped.

She jumped. Then scowled at him.

"What?"

"Here," Logan said, holding out the rusty nail. "Take this transmitter to the animal shelter. When you get there, find a secluded place for us to transport to."

Aggy took the nail and scrutinized it skeptically. "This is the transmitter?"

"Yes. It transmits a sound that the alien homes in on, so she can transport us."

"Logan, this is a *nail*."

"It's a transmitter," the alien in the corner said, her throat light illuminating the shed briefly.

Aggy's cloud of confusion broke enough to let in a frightening thought.

"So you really are . . ." she said haltingly. "You're from a . . . ?"

"Yes," the alien said. "I am from another planet. Don't be afraid. I won't harm you."

Aggy began to lean forward for a better look at this creature, then, as if thinking better of it, straightened up.

"I'll bring you up to date later," Logan said. "Right now we must get to the shelter. It's our only way of rescuing Festus and the other stolen dogs."

"Where are they?" Aggy asked. "Who has them?"

Logan stepped past her and tucked the rest of the clothes he'd taken from his house, including his rubber boots, into her bike's basket.

"Ride to the shelter," he told her. "Don't stop for any reason. Don't talk to anyone. Try to stay out of sight."

"What are the clothes for?"

"It's not important. You must get moving. Every second we wait increases our chances of failure."

Aggy didn't move. She seemed stuck, stupefied, paralyzed.

"He's right," the alien said. "You should go now."

"Okay," Aggy said, faking a strong voice and edging away. "She talks like a phone robot," she said to Logan out of the corner of her mouth as she climbed on her bike.

"Go," Logan said.

"Okay, I'm going, I'm going." She peddled unsteadily away.

"What did she have on her head?" the alien asked Logan.

"A helmet," Logan said. "To protect her if she has an accident on her bike. That was a bike she was riding."

"I see. Is she your friend as well as your co-operative?"

"Yes. And she's the rightful owner of one of the dogs on your ship."

"Oh," the alien said. "We'll have to get it back to her then."

"Yes," Logan said. "We will."

The alien peered out the slats of the shed.

"I can't see much of it from here, or at night, but your planet seems quite beautiful."

"How is it different from yours?" Logan asked.

"The air is so thin. And clear. I feel so much heavier."

"I felt lighter on the ship, in your air," Logan said.

"Your view of the stars is different, of course."

"Does your planet have moons?"

"It does. Only one, though. How many does yours have?"

"One. We call it the moon."

"So do we," said the alien, smiling.

"I suppose we should be quiet, huh?" Logan said. "We don't want anyone to hear us. Or see your throat light."

"Yes, you're right."

"Can your boss really bring me back anytime he wants?"

"I would have to help him. I would have to send you."

"Would you, ma'am?"

"I am obliged to by my contract. I agreed to do what I am told."

"So you would?"

The alien looked away. "We should be quiet now."

They sat in silence as the sky turned darker.

They admired the waxing gibbous moon when it rose up out of the trees.

"She should be at the shelter soon, ma'am," Logan whispered.

"Then we should be going. Ready?"

"Ready," Logan said, and he blacked out.

33. Twenty-two Dogs

Logan did not see, hear, or feel anything during the ultrasonic transport. The world went black for a split second, then he was somewhere else. He would have preferred some special effects: flashing lights, whooshing or zinging sounds, a twirling or flying or falling sensation.

"Logan!" Aggy was calling from somewhere.

He quickly ducked behind a low bush. "Over here, Aggy!" he called. "Over here!"

"Where?" Aggy asked, peddling her bike closer. She saw the alien standing beside the bush, pointing to where Logan was hiding.

"Throw me the clothes!" Logan said.

Aggy removed the wad of clothes from her basket and lobbed them over the bush. Logan put them on, then stood and handed the alien his mom's skirt and sweatshirt. The alien merely stared at them.

"Help her, will you, Aggy?" Logan asked. "She doesn't know how to put them on."

"I don't need to put them on," the alien said. "We don't wear clothes on my planet."

"You're not cold?" Aggy asked."

"No," the alien said.

Logan shrugged. "Then forget it." He tossed the clothes back to Aggy.

"Why doesn't her mouth move when she talks?" Aggy asked.

"I'll tell you later," Logan said, then turned to the alien. "The dogs are in there, ma'am," he said, indicating the white, wooden, one-story building beside them. Barking and whining could be heard coming from inside.

"There are twenty-two of them. Ten are female."

"How does she know that?" Aggy asked.

"The aliens can hear higher frequencies than us," Logan explained. "Like dogs."

"Why are we here?" Aggy asked. "Is Festus in there?"

"No," Logan said. "I talked the alien into swapping shelter dogs for the stolen dogs."

Aggy looked at the alien. "You stole my dog?"

"Not her," Logan said. "She took care of the dogs aboard the spaceship. Her boss stole them."

"I'm sorry," the alien said to Aggy. "Which is yours?"

"Black with a white belly," Logan said. "Short legs. Old."

"White at the tip of his tail?" the alien asked.

"That's him!" Aggy said, her eyes tearing. "Can you get him back?"

The alien was about to answer, but suddenly she pivoted her head, as if she had heard something.

"I have to go," she said, and opened her mouth. Her tongue tightened.

"Go? You can't *go*!" Logan pleaded.

But she was gone.

"No!" Logan shrieked, shaking his fists at the sky. "You can't leave! Come back! Come *back*!"

"Why did she do that?" Aggy asked. "Isn't she going to help us?"

"He must have ordered her back to the spaceship!" Logan said, then again addressed the night sky. "You promised!"

And the alien returned.

"She's back!" Aggy said.

Logan's fury subsided. He squinted at the alien. It was grinning, but only on one side of its mouth.

"It's not her. It's him," Logan said.

"Very good," the alien said. "You can tell us apart."

"Only by your expressions," Logan said. "Yours is either angry or sneaky."

"This is the boss?" Aggy asked. "The dognapper?"

"Pleased to meet you," the alien said. "Though actually I've seen and heard you many times before."

"You stole Festus!" she said. "Give him back!"

"Easy now," the alien said. "One thing at a time."

"Why are you here, sir?" Logan asked. "That

wasn't in our plan. You were supposed to stay on the ship and send the dogs to my house."

"Yes, *after* I was certain of the existence of this animal shelter you spoke of, and *after* it was established it held more dogs than I stole."

"Well, this is it," Logan said, waving a hand at the shelter. "I'm sure you can count the dogs inside by their voices. Twenty-two."

"Quite right," the alien said. "Twenty-two. Which is more than the eleven we have on board the ship."

"Right," Logan said. "But before you transport them up, sir, we have to go to my house and you have to return the dogs, like you promised."

"How will we get there?" the alien said. "Your little friend here has the transmitter."

Aggy patted her pants pocket, the one with the rusty nail in it. "I still have it," she said.

"That's true, sir," Logan said, thinking quickly. "Aggy will bike back to my house."

"I'm afraid we cannot go to your house before I transport the dogs to the ship," the alien said.

"Why not?" Logan asked.

"Because I'm going to transport them to the ship now." The alien opened his mouth wide.

"No!" Logan screamed. "You promised, sir! We shook hands and tapped noses. . . ."

The alien vanished, as did the barking from the shelter.

34. Giving the Boss the Business

"I say we call nine-one-one," Aggy said to Logan, who was sitting on the handlebars of her bike as she pedaled.

"No one will believe us," Logan said over his shoulder. "No one can help us. We don't have any other choice but to go to my house and hope he keeps his promise."

"Why would he?" Aggy said. "He has everything he wanted. He has all the dogs."

"But he tapped noses with me."

"Stop with the tapping noses, will you?"

"So far he's kept his word. The deal was the dogs and I get sent home and he takes the shelter dogs. He took the shelter dogs, but he left me here. Now he'll return the dogs."

"They're probably shooting across the universe in their spaceship as we speak!"

"I disagree."

"Will you stop tipping?" Aggy yelled as the bike started to wobble. "You're going to make me crash."

"I'm not trying to! Stop hitting bumps!"

"I can barely see the road ahead of me, with you in my face! And it's dark!"

"Just hurry up, will you?" Logan said. "Nothing can happen till we get the transmitter there."

"I'm hurrying, I'm hurrying. I can just imagine how freaked out my parents are right now. Your mom sure is."

"Everything will be fine when we get home," Logan said, though he wasn't at all sure this was true.

The alley was darker now, due to the kitchen lights along it having been turned off, dinnertime having come and gone. Logan walked quietly beside Aggy, who walked her bike. The lights were on in Logan's living room. The rest of the house was dark. Logan assumed this meant his mother had returned, but he couldn't be sure she was still there. If she was, he thought, she might not be alone. There might even be police officers in the house, investigating his disappearance.

He wished he'd arranged a different drop-off point.

"Maybe we should just go in," Aggy whispered to him as they hunkered down behind the backyard fence.

"Don't scream," a robotic voice said from the other side of the fence, amid a golden, glowing light.

Aggy almost did, but Logan clamped his hand over her mouth.

"It's the alien," he whispered, then released her.

"Which one?" Aggy whispered back.

Logan slowly swung the gate open, and they stole into the backyard. They found the female alien hidden in a dark corner, hugging a tree. Logan leaned in close.

"It's her," he whispered to Aggy, then to the

alien he said, "We have to be careful, ma'am. There are people in the house. You don't want anyone to see you."

She nodded.

"Did your boss send you here, ma'am?" Logan whispered. "Is he going to send back the dogs?"

The alien shook her head.

"No?" Aggy gasped.

The alien shook her head again, then hung it in shame.

"Can you beam the dogs here yourself?" Logan asked.

"I could, but he would simply transport them back again."

"Why are you here then, ma'am?" Logan asked. .

The alien placed her hand over her neck, over the light. Golden light streamed between her fingers. "He's preparing to leave your planet."

"See?" Aggy said to Logan.

"But I told him I was coming here," the alien went on, "and I would stay till he returned the dogs."

"But isn't that against your contract, ma'am?" Logan asked.

"I won't be following his orders from now on."

"Good for you!" Aggy said.

"Can't he just beam you up?" Logan asked.

"No," the alien said. "Our kind can resist. Refuse. It would be awful if we couldn't."

"What if he leaves you here?" Aggy asked. "How will you get home?"

The alien shook her head.

"That's a big risk you're taking," Aggy said. "Just for our dogs."

"He needs me," the alien said. "He can't do everything by himself. He'll send the dogs down."

"I hope you're right," Logan said.

The alien opened her mouth wide.

"Is that him?" Logan asked.

She closed it. "Yes. He's demanding I return or he will leave without me."

"You have to go then," Aggy said. "You can't stay here. I know Festus will be in good hands with you. Or good fins, or whatever."

The alien smiled but shook her head.

Logan wracked his brain, trying to think of

a solution. The longer he couldn't, the more frustrated he became; the more frustrated he became, the more angry he got. He felt he was about to blow his top.

"Abyssin, Aleena, Amanin, Ansionians," he said.

"What are you saying, Logan?"

"I'm alphabetizing the aliens from *Star Wars*," he said. "Anomid, Annoo dat, Anx, Anzati . . . It calms me down when I'm angry . . . Aqualish, Aramandi, Arcona . . ."

"Well, stop it."

"I have it!" Logan said a little too loudly.

"Shhh!" Aggy hissed.

Logan ignored her and spoke to the alien. "Tell your boss to be sure he scoops up the dogs' poop every day. The poop of thirty-six dogs, that is. Every day. And their pee, too. And tell him he has to feed and water them as well. They're his responsibility now. If he doesn't take care of them, they won't survive the trip home."

Aggy and the alien stared at him, stumped.

"Well, do it," Logan said crossly. "Tell him!"

"He probably heard you, but I will tell him,"

the alien said, and opened her mouth.

"How is that going to help?" Aggy asked Logan.

"Bosses don't like to do stuff like that," Logan said. "That's why they're bosses."

The alien shut her mouth.

"What did he say?" Logan asked.

The alien shook her head. "Nothing."

"What did you expect him to say?" Aggy asked. "'Okay. You win. You can have your dogs back'?"

Logan shrugged.

"That's him again," the alien said, gaping again.

Pickles appeared on the lawn.

35. A Polite Young Man

Pickles shook a few times, as if she were wet, then ran across the grass to the alien.

"Look at that!" Aggy said. "She likes you!"

Another dog appeared, this one small with a pushed-in face and long hair. Logan thought it looked like Chloe, and worried it would start yapping like Chloe and bring his mom—and maybe the police—outside before all the dogs were back and the extraterrestrial safely returned to her spaceship. But, like Pickles, it kept its snout shut and ran to the alien.

Next was Ollie. Then a pug. Then a pit bull. Then Nilla, the puppy. They all remained silent, and all rushed to the alien. The rest of the dogs arrived, one by one, and all followed the same routine. All, that is, but one. This one was a fat old beagle/dachshund mix that looked like a cow, and went straight to Aggy.

Aggy hugged him and rubbed him and kissed him all over his face. Festus thumped his tail on the ground like a drumstick on a drum.

The porch light switched on. Logan's mom leaned against the glass of the window, her hand shading her eyes.

"Logan?" she called.

"I have to go," the alien said.

"Yes, you should," Logan said, his heart racing and sinking at the same time.

"Thank you so much," Aggy said.

"Yes. Thank you, ma'am," Logan added.

"Such a polite, clever, and dedicated young man," the alien said, her golden light glowing. "And such a dear friend your co-operative is."

Then she opened her mouth and was gone.

"Logan?"

His mom had opened the back door and was standing on the porch, still shading her eyes.

Logan glanced at Aggy, unsure how she would view a boy his age doing what he really wanted to do, then went ahead and did it: he flew across the yard and into his mother's arms.

His mom laughed and cried and peppered him with kisses, all the while saying, "I have been scared out of my wits!" "We looked everywhere!" "Where have you been?" and "Do you know what I'm going to do to you once I get over being relieved?"

Finally, realizing they weren't alone, she said, "Where did all these dogs come from?"

The animals rushed up to them, frantic for attention. Except for Festus, that is.

"They're the dognapped dogs," Logan said. "We found them."

"Is that Aggy?" his mom asked.

Aggy stepped out of the shadows, Festus at her heel.

"It's me, Jenny," she said.

"Your mom called. She's beside herself with worry."

"I was helping Logan. With the dogs."

"You found all the missing dogs?" Logan's mom asked. "Just the two of you? Because I could have sworn there was someone else with you. Someone . . . taller."

Aggy looked to Logan.

"It was one of the aliens, Mom," he said. "The nice one. She helped us."

His mom's brow wrinkled, then relaxed. "And you two got the dogs back."

"That's right," Logan said. "The Canine Rescue Unit got them back."

"The *Intergalactic* Canine Rescue Unit, you mean," Aggy said.

"Right," Logan said. "You do believe us, don't you, Mom?"

His mom exhaled, long and slow. Her whole body loosened. Her mouth opened into a generous smile. All her teeth showed.

"Of course I believe you," she said.

"The boss alien was wrong then," Logan said. "He said human adults don't listen to kids. They just humor us."

His mom squeezed him. "How he ever got to be boss, I'll never know."

36. Returning the Stolen Goods

The Crew met at Aggy's house the next morning.

"We found Pickles, ma'am," Logan said into Aggy's cell phone.

"My Pickles?" Trudy answered.

"We'll bring her over soon," Logan said.

"Oh, bless you, my boy! Bless you!"

"All in a day's work for the Intergalactic Canine Rescue Unit, ma'am."

He hung up, consulted another of his LOST DOG flyers, then dialed Lily, Ollie's owner. After he talked to her, he called another dog owner, then another, and on and on until he came to one with a picture of a lean, white, short-haired dog with a curled tail named Cowboy that read IF FOUND, PLEASE CALL MATTHIAS SARRIS.

"That must be Darius's dog!" Thatcher said. "His dad's name is Mr. Sarris, remember?"

Logan had not known the man's name when he found the flyer. He didn't learn it till just before the alien abducted him.

"We don't need to call then," Logan said. "We can just bring Cowboy over."

"You can apologize to Mr. Sarris for calling him an alien and a dog thief," Aggy added.

Logan flinched. "Yeah, I guess I could."

The last flyer was not about a lost dog. Logan called the number printed on it.

"Hello?" a voice said on the phone.

"Is this Helene?" Logan asked.

"Yes, it is. Who's calling?"

"My name is Logan Lonergan, ma'am, and I found your wheelchair."

"You did? Where?"

"In a cave, by Ketchoklam Park."

"In a cave?"

"Yes, ma'am. May I have your address, please, so I can return it?"

Logan scribbled down the address.

"Thank you, ma'am," he said. "We'll be there soon. Good-bye."

He hung up and said to the Crew, "Let's return these stolen goods to their rightful owners."

"Can I ride in the wheelchair?" Thatcher asked. "I'd really like a turn in it. I haven't had a turn yet. Please? Please please?"

"I told you before, Thatcher," Logan said. "No."

Everyone had brought as many leashes and collars as they could find at home and had attached them to the ten remaining rescued dogs. (Aggy left Festus at home as Logan had done with Bubba.) Each operative took three dogs except Logan, who took one, Ollie.

"I need the other hand to operate the joystick," he said, and demonstrated by pushing it forward.

Ollie yelped as the chair zoomed forward.

"Come on, you guys!" Logan called. "Keep up."

Thatcher, Kian, and Aggy, and the nine dogs they were tethered to, did their best.

"Did you guys tell your parents about the aliens?" Aggy asked as the trio of dogs she held tugged her in three different directions.

"I didn't," Kian said. "They would never believe me."

"I never believe you, dude," Thatcher said. "You're never serious."

"I'm always serious," Kian said, with a serious expression.

"See?" Thatcher said.

"I was busting to tell my parents," Aggy said. "But it just wouldn't come out of my mouth. It sounded too crazy."

"I told my mom, and she sent out a mass e-mail to all her friends about it," Logan said.

"I bet they all think she's joking," Aggy said. "Or nuts."

"Who cares?" Thatcher said. "It's true, isn't it? Logan really did get abducted by aliens, and he really did rescue the dogs. Right?"

"Right," Logan said.

"I sure wish I could have seen the aliens," Thatcher said, tossing back his hair. "I wish they had abducted me and beamed me up to the spaceship."

"I'll bean you," Kian said. "Here, let me bean

you," and he rapped Thatcher's skull with his knuckles.

"Ow! That hurt!" Thatcher said. "I said 'beam,' not 'bean.'"

He reached out to bean Kian's skull in return, but Kian ducked and, in trying to run away, got tangled up in his dogs' leashes.

"Aha!" Thatcher said, and leaped on top of him.

"Apes," Aggy said.

When they neared Patrice's house, Kian asked, "Isn't that where your babysitter lives, Logan?"

"She's not my babysitter," Logan answered sternly.

"Ollie's owner, Lily, lives across the street, right?" Aggy asked.

"In that house," Logan said, pointing.

He parked the wheelchair in front and led Ollie up the walk. The others stayed at the curb with their dogs.

"Intergalactic Canine Rescue Unit, ma'am," Logan said when Lily opened the door. "We're returning your dog, as promised."

"Ollie!" the woman squealed, scooping up her puffball of a pet. "Oh, Ollie! I missed you so! Yes! Yes, I did!"

"I'm going to need the collar and leash back, ma'am," Logan said.

"Oh, of course," Lily said, and unbuckled it. "Now wait here a moment and I'll get my purse. You have a reward coming. . . ."

"Not necessary, ma'am," Logan said. "We didn't do it for money. Rescuing dogs is our duty. Now if you'll excuse me, we have more dogs to return to their owners."

Lily looked out at the pack of other dogs as if she hadn't noticed them before, and a confused look came over her face.

"Good-bye, ma'am," Logan said, and walked away, the leash and empty collar in his hand.

37. Dog Planet

Darius opened the door.

"Is your father at home?" Logan asked.

"Cowboy!" Darius said, looking past Logan at his dog. He was tugging at his leash, his curled tail wagging furiously. Thatcher let go of the leash and Cowboy bounded into Darius's arms.

"Is your father at home?" Logan asked again, louder.

"Give him a minute, Logan," Aggy whispered. "He's excited to see his dog."

Logan peered inside the house. "Hello? Mr. Sarris?"

"He isn't home," Darius said, continuing to lavish attention on his dog. "He works on Saturdays."

"Wow," Thatcher said. "You're here by

your*self*? At your age? At *our* age?"

"Why is that a big deal?" Kian said. "We leave Chloe alone all the time, and she's only three."

"Who's Chloe?" Darius asked.

"His mom's yappy little dog," Thatcher said, nudging Kian with his shoulder.

Kian shoved him back. Hard.

"Ow!" Thatcher said.

"Anyway, Logan, thanks for bringing back Cowboy," Darius said. "Where did you find him?"

"On an alien spaceship," Thatcher said, throwing Kian an elbow. "Logan was abducted. The aliens had stolen a whole bunch of dogs."

"Really?" Darius asked, looking doubtful.

"Really," said Kian, elbowing Thatcher.

"We've returned all the dogs we rescued except this one," Thatcher said to Darius, and pointed at the puppy, Nilla. "Want to come with us and help us find its owner?"

"Yeah, sure," Darius said. "I just need to call my dad and tell him." He pulled a cell phone out of his pocket.

"Wow," Thatcher said again.

"'*Wow!*'" Kian mocked, then walked away.

"What's up with you?" Thatcher asked, following him. "I just think the guy is cool. You're still my best friend!"

"Dad?" Darius said into the phone. "Guess what? They found Cowboy! Those kids. Logan and his friends. . . . Yeah, him."

"Can I talk to Mr. Sarris, please?" Logan asked.

"He wants to talk to you, Dad," Darius said. He listened to the answer, then looked at Logan and said, "He doesn't want to talk to you."

"Give it," Logan said, holding out his hand.

Darius handed the phone to him.

"Hello, Mr. Sarris, sir," Logan said into it. "I wanted to apologize. I was wrong. You weren't the alien. I found the real one and got your dog back. No need to thank me. Here's your son." And he handed the phone back to Darius.

"Why don't we check the telephone poles around Sandwiches?" Aggy asked. "Maybe the lady with the puppy hung up a flyer by now."

"We need to stop at Helene's first and return the wheelchair," Logan said.

"Can I ride it over there?" Thatcher asked.

"I haven't had a turn yet, and we're bringing it back . . ."

Logan sighed, then relented.

Helene also tried to give Logan a reward, but again he refused.

"All in the line of duty, ma'am," he said, and walked away.

"Yeah, money?" Kian said. "Who needs it?"

"Are we still going to be the Intergalactic Canine Rescue Unit after we return this puppy?" Thatcher asked. "Will our work be done? Do we have to move on?"

Logan shot him a weary look. "Thatcher, are you naive enough to believe that those were the only aliens on Earth? If they were, the chances of our finding them would be astronomical. No, there are others on our planet, and no doubt some of them will want to steal our dogs. The Intergalactic Canine Rescue Unit will remain active until every one of them is thwarted and sent on their way."

Thatcher smiled a wide, beaming smile. "The I-Crew rules!" he shouted, and pumped his fists in the air.

When they reached Sandwiches, they found the weekly farmers market in full swing.

"Oh, right," Aggy said. "It's Saturday."

"My parents are probably here," Thatcher said. "They always go to the market."

"Mine, too," said Kian.

"My dad works Saturdays," Darius said.

"You said that already," Kian said.

The street had been closed off to traffic and was filled with booths selling vegetables, jewelry, fresh salmon, honey, and other goods. People carrying baskets were milling about, talking and shopping, and, on the library's lawn, young children were chasing one another around, yelling and squealing. Logan knew many of them, having lived his whole life in Nelsonport. Many people said hello, to him and to his friends.

They ran into Thatcher's parents, and Kian's, but successfully slipped away from them and their boring adult conversations.

They also bumped into their teacher, Nathan, standing in front of one farmer's stand. He pointed at the lettuces and peppers and said, dramatically, "Produce!"

"Very funny, Nathan," Aggy said, rolling her eyes.

There were plenty of people with dogs as well, including a few of the dogs the Crew had rescued. Lily was there with Ollie, for example.

"Now I wish I'd brought Festus with me," Aggy said.

"I totally wish I had Bear," Thatcher said.

"I'm glad I don't have Chloe," Kian said.

"If I had Bubba, she'd probably just lie down on the ground and fart," Logan said.

"At least we live on a planet that has dogs," Aggy said.

"True," Logan said.

"I have Cowboy," Darius said. "Anybody want to play Fetch with us?"

"I do, Darius!" Kian said. "I do!"

"'I do!'" mocked Thatcher, then he pulled Kian aside and asked, "Do you like him better than me?"

Suddenly, a young woman let out a screech and started running toward them, her arms out in front of her, an enormous smile on her face.

"Nilla!" she called. "Oh, Nilla! My baby!"

She hugged her dog as Darius had, and Lily, and Trudy, and Aggy: tightly, happily, tearily.

"How did you find him?" she asked, looking up.

"We're the Intergalactic Canine Rescue Unit, ma'am," Logan said. "It's what we do."

Patrick Jennings

is the author of many popular novels for middle-schoolers, including *Guinea Dog, Lucky Cap, We Can't All Be Rattlesnakes,* and *Faith and the Electric Dogs.* He won the 2011 Washington State Scandiuzzi Children's Book Award for *Guinea Dog,* which is also nominated for the following state lists: Colorado 2011–2012 Children's Book Award, New Hampshire 2011–2012 Great Stone Face Book Award, and the Kansas 2012–2013 William Allen White Children's Book Award. He lives in a small seaport town in Washington State.

You can visit him online at www.patrickjennings.com.